Y0-ABM-020

The Puca were a peculiar lot. They often passed as human, but anyone who knew them well could spot the flickering of the ears, the green gleam in the eyes. What humans couldn't spot or follow was the otherworldly logic of their minds, a shatteringly profound logic that could (would?) doom mankind.

Worse still, the seven (or was it six?) Puca children were deadlier than their parents.

THE REEFS OF EARTH

R.A. LAFFERTY

A BERKLEY MEDALLION BOOK

published by

BERKLEY PUBLISHING CORPORATION

Copyright © 1968, by R.A. Lafferty

All rights reserved

Published by arrangement with the author

All rights reserved which includes the right
to reproduce this book or portions thereof in
any form whatsoever. For information address

Berkley Publishing Corporation
200 Madison Avenue
New York, N.Y. 10016

SBN 425-03565-4

*BERKLEY MEDALLION BOOKS are published by
Berkley Publishing Corporation
200 Madison Avenue
New York, N.Y. 10016*

BERKLEY MEDALLION BOOK ® TM 757,375

Printed in the United States of America

Berkley Medallion Edition, NOVEMBER, 1977

SECOND PRINTING

CONTENTS

1   To Slay the Folks and Cleanse the Land   1

2   And Leave the World a Reeking Roastie   11

3   High Purpose of the Gallant Band   23

4   And Six Were Kids, and One a Ghostie.   35

5   A Child's a Monster Still Uncurled   43

6   The World's a Trap, and None Can Quit It—   53

7   The "Strife Dulanty" With the World   65

8   Was Mostly That They Didn't Fit It.   77

9   No Setting For the Gallant Brood   89

10   In Sacred Groves of Yew or Lindens   99

11   They Found a Hold More Near Their Blood   111

12   A Mountainful of Murdered Indians   119

13   In Brazen Clash of Helm and Greave   137

14   Fit Subject For Heroic Chantey   149

15   The Battle Joined That Could But Leave   159

16   Or Altered World or Dead Dulanty.   173

THE REEFS OF EARTH

1

To Slay the Folks and Cleanse the Land

Nowhere in all the worlds was there a more fearless family than the Dulantys. And the Dulanty children had such towering intrepidity as to leave even their elders gasping.

Then what was it on this one world—the one on which the children themselves happened to be born—that so scared them?

Listen, people, creatures, devices, entities, *it was the meanest world in all the universes!* It'd have spooked you too.

We don't know why anyone would want to visit it. We sure don't know why anyone would want to be born on it. But the children hadn't been able to control their place of birth.

Sometimes traveling people will be talking together. They will say how good it is in some places and how bad it is in others. And, sooner or later, one of them is bound to mention it. "Talk about really being out in the boondocks!" he will say, "there's a little planet named Earth—"

There were six children, or seven if you counted Bad John. At that time they lived in the Big Shanty, and they told stories at night. It was their way of exorcising all the bleakness of Earth. It was whistling in the dark. A place like Earth will wilt the flesh off your bones unless you can make fun of it, or treat its persons and places as no worse than ghosts and ghost places.

This is the story that Elizbeth told:

"There was this picture of a man that looked at you. A Puca man and woman had just come to Earth, and they thought they should have some Earth things around their house so people wouldn't suspect them. They bought the picture and hung it up in the hall downstairs, and went upstairs to bed. But they couldn't sleep for thinking about the spooky thing.

" 'It bothers me the way the man in the picture looks at one with those green eyes,' the woman said. 'They're not green, they're brown,' the man said. 'Damn this crazy world where eyerything's woolly!' 'You are woolly yourself,' the woman said, 'his eyes are green. Let's go down and see.' They went down to see, and the man in the picture's eyes were brown, but the woman knew they had been green the first time. They went back upstairs to bed.

" 'We shouldn't have bought it,' the woman said. 'He looks like a madman with all that red hair.' 'It isn't red, it's black,' the man said. 'Let's go down and settle this thorny business.' They went down to see, and it was black; but the woman knew it had been red the first time. Things like that shiver you when they keep happening. 'I've known haunted houses,' the woman said, 'but this is a haunted world.' They went back upstairs and went to bed.

" 'Another thing I don't like is that dog,' the woman said when the man was just drifting off to sleep. 'I'm afraid of that dog in the picture.' 'There isn't any dog in that picture,' the man said. 'What's the matter with you

2

anyhow? You're as silly as an Earth woman. Let's go down and see.'

" 'You go see,' the woman said. 'I've been down twice, and I know there *is* a dog in the picture.' Then she said a Bagarthach verse:

" *'I'm turning livid in this bog,*
This woolly world that spooks and spites you.
You'll find that picture's got a dog!
I hope the blinking bugger bites you!''

"Boy, she sure shouldn't have said a Bagarthach verse like that! But she was sleepy and not thinking very hard. The man went downstairs. And in a minute there was a growling and gnashing and tearing. The woman went down then to see what in pumpkin pickers' heaven the racket was all about.

"And the man was dead with his throat bitten through. And the dog was back in the picture and his mouth was foamed with blood. 'See! I was right,' the woman said, 'there *was* a dog in the picture. Remind me to get rid of that thing in the morning, Albert.' She forgot for the moment that Albert was dead with his throat bitten through and wouldn't be able to remind her of it. She shouldn't have used a Bagarthach verse when she was just kidding. Earth things are so dumb that they don't know when to obey a Bagarthach and when not to."

That was Elizabeth's story. Elizabeth was nine years old, the oldest of the seven children (or the six, if you don't count Bad John). She was as beautiful as an Earth child.

There is no use kidding about it. The Puca themselves are not handsome. And the people of Earth (they deserve that, they have so little else going for them) are. Some-

3

times they will have a Puca child to be born good-looking. Witchy (Elizabeth's mother) was born so and remained so. Veronica (the mother of some of the children) had been born so and had given it up. Mostly, the Puca, if they happen to be born of a pretty appearance and face, are able to maintain it while they are young. But with the coming of maturity, the shattering profundity of the developing Puca character will smash and bevanish that pretty mask and replace it with a deeper face, intricate and ugly and of a high humor.

Elizabeth was the best-looking of them all. But for the gleam in her eyes and the way she flicked her ears and crinkled her nose when she talked, nobody could have told that she wasn't an Earth child.

All the children were brothers and sisters and cousins.

This is the story that Charles told:

"There was a Puca man who had to be on Earth a little while. He was a traveling salesman, and he didn't notice that in his new contract one year they had added Earth to his territory. 'Boy, isn't that something?' he said. 'I bet I read the fine print next year.' Well, he came to Earth and he walked all day and didn't see a good customer anywhere. And just at night he came to a country hotel. The hotel man was greedy like all people on Earth, and he charged him a dollar for a room. So he went up to his room (the Puca man, not the hotel man) and locked the door, and answered a couple letters from the home office, and turned out the light and went to bed. And that is when things started to happen.

"Everything on Earth is either alive or spooked or both. The wood that they build the rooms out of is alive and it squeaks and whispers and coughs. The air is full of stuff, and there are whole multitudes of creatures living in the walls. Then it went Bang and the man came out of bed scared to turn the light on. But it was already turned on, and nobody could have turned it on but himself. He went to see, and the door was still locked. 'I'm too scared to turn the light off now,' he said. 'I'll go to sleep with it on.' He started to get back in bed and he saw that there was already somebody in the bed. 'He looks kind of like the hotel man,' the Puca man said, 'and he looks kind of like me. We don't look anything alike, but I will just be damned if I can say which one of us it is lying there. Whichever one of us it is, he's got his throat cut and he sure is dead.' It was the hotel man that was dead, though. Those Earth people look real mean when they're dead— you can always tell them that way. The Puca man was so scared that he unlocked the door and pulled it open so fast that the doorknob came off in his hand. He ran out of the hotel, and when he looked back, the hotel was gone. 'But I know I didn't dream it,' he said, 'because I still got the doorknob in my hand.' Then he looked down and the doorknob had turned into a rock. After that, when he traveled, he went by train even if it cost more, and he didn't stop at any more of those little country hotels.''

Charles was eight. There were seven children: Elizabeth, Charles, Helen, Peter, Dorothy, John, and Bad John. Mostly they told stories on the nights of heavy thunder, and in the Crow Creek country in the early autumn it was heavy thunder almost every night.

This is the story that Helen told:
''There was a man who came back to his home town after a long time. He got off the train at the town, and walked down the tracks to the junction where he lived that was so little that the train didn't even stop there. He saw a man named Silly Jimmy sitting on a pile of ties, and talked

to him. Silly Jimmy didn't seem to be in his wits, but then the man remembered that Silly Jimmy never had been in his wits. The man walked on home and saw his folks and told them that he was glad to get back to Earth to see them again even if it was a miserable place. And then he told them that he had just been talking to Silly Jimmy out by the pile of ties.

" 'But Silly Jimmy died a long time ago,' they told him. 'We wrote you about it, how the train ran over him.' And the man remembered that they did. They had even made a Bagarthach verse about it:

" 'The engine spattered him like tar,
And broke his bones and burst his belly.
We gathered Jimmy in a jar.
Hey, pass the Silly Jimmy Jelly!'

"So the man went outdoors again to where Silly Jimmy had been sitting and whittling, and there were fresh whittles on the ground. Silly Jimmy had been whittling whether he was dead or not. That's the way things are with Earth people. You think one of them's dead, and then you'll run into him again."

Helen was six years old, and the smallest of them all.

This is the story that Peter told:

"There was a little girl that died and went to Hell, but she kept saying, 'I didn't do it, it was my sister that did it, if you let me out of this damned place—' (Hey, that's kind of funny!)—'I'll prove that I was the one that didn't do it.' 'How would you prove it?' the guard asked. (He wasn't a Puca, none of the people who run it down there are Pucas, they're all from Earth or from Ifreann.) 'I'd scare my sister into admitting it,' the girl said. 'All right,' said the

6

guard, 'but no tricks.'

"They went back to her house and up to her sister's room who was named Clarissa. 'I'm Alice's ghost,' said Alice. 'I came back to scare you into admitting that you were the one that stole the money so you can go to Hell instead of me.' 'Hello, Alice,' said Clarissa. 'Hello, sir, are you the guard? Then you must know what a liar she is. If you will step outside, sir, I will take care of my sister. She must be punished for telling lies.'

"So the guard stepped out of the room for a minute, and mean Clarissa (she was the one that stole the money, all right) shook Alice till her head nearly fell off and she dropped her ghost sheet. Then Clarissa put on the ghost sheet and scared Alice till she lay on the bed and howled.

"The guard came back in. 'Did you scare her into admitting it?' he asked Clarissa who was wrapped in Alice's ghost sheet and he thought she was Alice. 'I sure did,' Clarissa said. 'Do you admit you stole it?' the guard asked Alice that he thought was Clarissa—they looked just alike. 'No, I do not,' Alice said, and she wasn't scared any more. 'Take her back and don't pay any attention to what she says because she's a liar.' So the guard took Clarissa back to Hell (he thought she was Alice), so everything was all right. A lot times, you can make everything work all right if you send just one person out of a bunch to Hell."

Peter was eight years old, and the funniest-looking of them all except John, and except Bad John, if you count him. Elizabeth and Charles and Helen looked like angels, or like handsome Earthlings. Their cousins Peter and Dorothy and John and Bad John looked like potato-faced goblins, like real Pucas. Witchy said that they had planned it that way, that some of the children should look like children of this place, and some of them should look like

7

the children back home.

But they all had those eyes that glowed like green coals. Look at them straight, and you'd hardly notice a thing. But look at them sideways accidentally sometimes, just catching them in the corner of your eye, and they'd scare the liver out of you.

This is the story that Dorothy told:

"There was a man that was run over by a train right outside here on the track that goes by the shanty. The train cut him up in little pieces when it ran over him. After that, he came back once a year and would stand in the middle of the track at night like he was made of fog. He swung a lantern that made about as much light as a lightning bug in a fruit jar. The first time, the engineer of the Flyer just barely saw him in time, and he hit the whistle and the brakes and scattered sparks for a quarter mile. Then they got out and couldn't find any pieces of that man.

"But after that, they got onto him, and went right through him without paying any attention. But one year the man stole a real live lantern and swung it, and the man was thicker than he used to be and made out of heavier fog. A train came down the tracks loud, but it was an old train that nobody had seen before. The train saw the man and switched onto the old track to miss him—it was the old track they don't use any more that runs right under our shanty. I was the only one awake to see it, and I made a sign or we'd all have been killed. The train hit the shanty with a noise like a big wind, and went right through without breaking it up. It was a ghost train too; it was the same train that killed the man the first time."

Dorothy was seven years old.

This is the story that John told:

"There was a boy and girl that got married. He was a good Puca boy, but she was an Earth girl, and you can't tell about them. They said that whichever one of them died first would come back and tell the other one what it was like. Then the man died and his name was William. But he didn't come back to tell her what it was like right away, so she married a man named Tom and her name was Polly. The first night they were married, someone came to the door, and Tom went to see who it was. Then he came back.

" 'He asked for you,' Tom said. 'He said to tell you that it sure is cold.' 'He must be the man selling coal,' Polly said. 'Tell him to leave a load.' After a while someone came to the door again, and Tom went. Then he came back. 'He asked for you,' Tom said. 'He said to tell you that it sure is dark.' 'He's probably the man selling kerosene,' Polly said. 'Tell him to leave a barrel for the lamps.'

"After a while somebody came to the door again, and Tom went. Then he came back. 'He asked for you,' Tom said. 'He said to tell you that it sure is lonesome.' 'Well, you go tell him that it isn't lonesome here,' Polly said, 'and it isn't cold, and it isn't dark. You tell him to be gone back to that hole where he belongs. I don't care any more how it is there.'

"Then a big wind came through the house and knocked Tom down dead. It blew so cold that it froze Polly stiff. It blew the house away and blew a hole in the ground and Polly fell down in it. The wind covered her up with dirt. Then William said, 'I knew you wanted to know what it was like, Polly.' "

John was six years old.

Last of all, it was Bad John's time to tell a story. But

nobody ever listened to Bad John's. He couldn't tell ghost stories, he could only tell people stories, and nobody cares about them.

After the stories, they would all go to bed in the old loft there and turn out the lights. Except Bad John, who didn't have any bed. Nobody knows where he went when the lights went out.

It was their way of defying that tricky place Earth. That place will hurt you if you let it get the hop on you. They spooked the Earth spooks away with their stories. They whistled in the dark.

Except Bad John, who couldn't whistle.

2

And Leave the World a Reeking Roastie

The Henry Dulanty and Frank Dulanty families were pilgrims on Earth, and had been in Lost Haven only six weeks when this disintegration begins. The way of their coming was this:

The double family had been on the move in two station wagons, a sideboard truck, and a van truck. Veronica drove one of the station wagons and had all the children with her. Witchy drove the other wagon, loaded with everything in the world. Henry in the sideboard truck had the furniture, and Frank in the van had the tools and shops of the several professions of the two brothers.

They stopped the four vehicles one noon in a quiet weed patch by the road, and Veronica brought out lunches for the ten of them. (Bad John is not numbered in the ten; he did not eat.)

Then an angry man appeared and barked at them and offered to bite them. Does anyone ever get over the shock of meeting the people of Earth? They make your hair rise up.

"We won't have our town dirtied up by strangers," the man said, "and you're the strangest clutch I ever saw."

"Where's any town?" Henry Dulanty asked sharply. A Puca man can't let an Earth man jump him like that.

"You're standing in the middle of Lost Haven," the man said.

Well, there *was* a town there, a shabby one, hidden by the weeds and thickets, and the Dulantys hadn't noticed it.

But Helen had this man pegged. She didn't like him at all. So she killed him with a Bagarthach verse crooned low:

> *"Old Crocker man, be belled and banged!*
> *You hound-dog hunk, we'll have you hounded!*
> *On else than gallows be you hanged!*
> *In else than water be you drownd-ed!"*

Say, Helen killed that man neat, even though it'd take him a few weeks to realize that he was dead.

"We won't harm your town, but we might harm you," Frank Dulanty said out loud to the man. "You go now. We go when we're ready."

The man went away, pale and jerky, as though he were the one who had been given a summons. His name was Crocker, and he was a mean one.

And half an hour later, as the Dulantys were getting ready to leave, a larger man came and barked at them in a louder manner.

"My man told you to leave," the big man said. "I don't know what you are, but you don't belong anywhere on God's green Earth. I'll boot the lot of you up the road if you're not gone just as quick as you can climb into those crates and fire off. I'm Coalfactor Stutgard, and I own this town."

"Let me kill this one," Peter whispered to the other children. Then he growled out a Bagarthach verse that would finish that man off forever:

> *"Too long, too late you steal and strut;*

Your bubble breaks, your grip relaxes!
Beware the under-studding, Stut!
Beware of jackals bearing axes!"

Peter got him too, as neat as Helen had had her prey. It's funny that when you kill a man, he's often the last one to know about it.

"We will stay," said Frank Dulanty. "Nobody can tell us to go."

"You can stay nowhere," Stutgard said. "I own every house in this town."

"We will stay," said Henry Dulanty, giving a solid echo to his brother. That man wasn't about to boot them up the road! Though a big man, he wasn't as big or as young as Henry Dulanty. So Stutgard left them, shaking with fury.

But the Dulantys were shaken also. It had happened to them dozens of times, and they never became inured to it. Earth people have a capacity for hatred, and it goes out of them like waves.

The Dulantys were always uneasy at these times. They *were* unusual-looking, and they knew it. They could, of course, have looked a little more like Earth people if they had wished to, but this day it just didn't seem worth the bother.

A little later, a man came to them furtively, and told them that Coalfactor Stutgard had lied. There was one house in town that he didn't own. The big ramshackle thing by the old railroad tracks belonged to an Indian lady who lived in Catoosa. So they unloaded and moved into the building. This was the Big Shanty.

Then Henry Dulanty drove the sideboard truck to Catoosa and rented the shanty from the Indian lady. He also bought a truckload of groceries, guessing that for a while nothing would be sold to them in Lost Haven.

So, they had stopped there out of stubbornness, as they would not be run off. They found the place, as they found every place, interesting. It was one of their jobs to find out about places.

Then a series of disasters struck them down, and they could not have moved on if they had wanted to.

The Dulantys were Irish according to one story that they told. They were French according to another. And they were something entirely different according to a story which they did not tell to Earth people.

Aye, but they were Puca! If you belong to Earth people you might not be familiar with the name of them. But you know the thing from before you were born! There is a little hackle-raising on both sides whenever the two people meet.

Whatever their descent, the Dulantys had a hard time getting along with the people of Earth, and it wasn't entirely the fault of the Earth people.

They had come to this fundament ten years earlier, the two Dulanty brothers newly married to the two Corcoran sisters. (Neither name is even a rough transliteration. There are not sufficient characters in Earth languages to transcribe the names they had at home.) They adopted Earth first names, and gave such to their children.

It was after coming to Earth that they sowed their seven children (Bad John is included in this count). The children were thus citizens of Earth if they wished to be. Moreover, it was believed that by their birth on Earth they would have immunity to Earth Allergy, that killing sickness.

"Earth is, after all, one of the four worlds," the Puca instructors had instructed them. "Earth people are, comical though it seems, our cousins in blood. So far, the blood between us has been bad blood. We send out picked young couples now. It is time we achieved accord with Earth. And, if not accord—ah—we believe it is time that *something* was done about the planet. Perhaps your own offspring will solve the problem intuitively. We frankly do not know what to do about a people so closely related to us and yet so alien to us.''

Well, the Dulantys (and a few others) had been working at the problem for ten years and more. They had *not* achieved accord.

Of the sisters, Veronica looked like an old potato, and Witchy was of an unearthly ('tis a Puca *abhacht*, and not a pun) beauty. But who can say which was the more beautiful where they came from?

They were not twins in age, Witchy having been born eleven months after Veronica. But Veronica swore that they were conceived on the same night, and she told an Aorach story that proved it.

(The Puca have but two art-forms, both of them verbal: the Bagarthach verse, and the Aorach story.) Veronica was mistress of the Aorach. She winked with her whole potato face when she told one of her stories to Earth people, and this is what she told of her getting and Witchy's:

"Papa had to get up at four in the morning to light the furnace at the brickyard. (It wasn't really a brickyard; it was where they made something else in another place, but you wouldn't understand that.) And Mama used to sit up all night playing cribbage (it was really another sort of game with another name, but we will call it cribbage) with Grandma. So Papa and Mama never got together, and year after year nature's purpose was defeated. But one night Mama got mad at Grandma for cheating, and she went to bed at one minute before four o'clock.

" 'Fulfillment!' Papa shouted with his ears and nose

twitching, 'now I will have offspring at last.' And one minute later the brickyard whistle blew, and Papa jumped up and put on his clothes and ran down to the brickyard to light the furnace. But he was uneasy in his mind.

" 'I wonder if it will be fruitful?' Papa said. 'A man should have more than one minute. Let the furnace be late for once!' So he ran back home to Mama. 'I had so little time, I'm not sure I did the job right,' he told Mama. 'You did it right,' Mama told him, 'and Veronica is already on the way.' 'Well, I'm going to do it all over again,' Papa said, and he did. That one was Witchy. But I was already on the way, so Witchy had to wait for eleven months after me to be born. That's why she's prettiest too. Papa took more time to her.

"It had to happen that way. That's the only time Mama and Papa ever got together. Papa still had to get up at four o'clock every morning to light the furnace at the brick-yard, and Mama and Grandma still played cribbage to-gether all night every night. Not that Grandma stopped cheating—she cheated till the day she died—but she was the only one Mama had to play cribbage with.''

An Earth doctor, who treated Veronica (unsuccess-fully) for Earth Allergy, told Veronica that such a thing was impossible, that twins could not be born eleven months apart. Imagine an Earth doctor trying to tell a mistress of the Aorach about something as fundamental as that.

"What does a country horse doctor know about how people work?'' she asked. "Especially our kind of people.''

The doctor grinned and rubbed his pate that time. He doctored humans and not horses, and he suspected that this was the trouble. He was fascinated also that Veronica saw and talked to a young son who had died and saw nothing unusual about it. Ah well, under her influence he could see the translucent boy also, but it *was* peculiar. Veronica was the real center of the two families.

Her sister Witchy was not so full a vessel as Veronica, but there was a lot in her. She had a curious effect on Earth men, she would set them panting and roaming like dogs. By Earth standards she was as beautiful as it was possible to be, and yet her appearance was just a thing she had once devised on the spur of the moment for the fun of it. She was really a burlesque of Earth beauty, but it was better than the original.

Henry Dulanty was tall and heavy. He looked like the ogre out of a fairy tale. He was. Earthers retain memory of earlier Pucas with such heads and hulks, and Earth children still dream about them. But the Earthers have lied about the ogre. He was the finest fellow you'd ever want to meet—in the daylight—not in the dark.

His brother Frank was tall and lean. All four of these parents had a striking goblinish strangeness in their appearance, though Witchy's was shimmered over with beauty.

Could they live on Earth? The adults did not expect to live to any great age, there seeming no way of avoiding Earth Allergy. But it was believed the children (being born here) would miss its main effect. They suffered it early and lightly, and they built up immunity to it.

The children did well. They were faster and more intelligent than Earth children, and half of them (as had been planned) looked like exceptionally handsome natives.

To learn custom and to be gainfully employed, and perhaps to decide if something could not be done with Earth; that was the assignment of the Dulantys. And they were very much on their own. They learned Earth custom by their own picaresque adventures.

The brothers were, for a while, gainfully employed as directors of a university that offered a total education in six weeks. The university failed, and for the most damnable detail! Who ever heard of having to have a permit to teach? It was like having to have a permit to breathe. They were employed as construction contractors. Quicksand fouled them up on one building. "There is something wrong with a world that has its continents so poorly supported!" Frank Dulanty swore. "The floor hasn't sunk more than a foot, and you want thirty thousand dollars for that?" But Henry always insisted that they pay off, and it made a hole in their fortunes.

They were employed in invention and mining and chemicals, in wheat and cattle and rice. They sold quite a few businesses that were going good, but nobody else would be able to make them go. Why, you can sing a Bagarthach verse over a business, and it will give it the semblance of prosperity long enough to sell it! It was easy as breaking sticks to make money at almost anything on this world. The Dulantys were loaded when they came to Lost Haven, but nobody knew that part of it.

But they moved on often. Wherever they stopped, there were always a few Earthers who called them goblins and buggers and neanderthals, and who hated them. It hurt. But whatever the brothers were occupied with, it was as though they were really on some other commission. And they were.

"There's been a mistake," Henry said once. "We were told that we would be in rapport with the Indian population and could easily set up a hegemony over them, but we find them a vanishing minority. I believe that our information was centuries out of date. An old folk-psyche analysis showed that the Indians would accept us readily

18

in spite of our difference. These things were suggestions only, however. We are to discover the present state of affairs for ourselves.''

The Dulantys *were* in rapport with the Indians, much more than with other people. There just weren't enough Indians left.

''There is an anomaly about the Earth people,'' Frank said. ''Though incapable of intelligence, they operate with frightening instinct. They are not able to think, but they are well able to act; and that is the danger to us. They have the unity and communication of the hive.

''They remind me of the fireflies on Mercator. You remember how the millions of those pseudoinsects would cluster on hillocks and trees and all pulsate with their light together? Those on one hill would answer the beacon flashes of those on another hill, and yet they were creatures so small that fifty of them could be heaped on the end of your finger—and blind. Ah, they spelled out derisive words with their pulsing light on the hillsides, but the individuals of them were ignorant of words and of concepts and of all else.

''The people of Earth are like that, which is why it is called the Haunted Planet. The Hive Ghost hovers over them invisible, and they feel it from one end of their communities to the other. We can handle Earth individuals as though they were furniture or stones, but we cannot handle the Hive Ghost that hangs over them. And it hates us, Henry.''

So the Dulantys traveled and raised their bright brood, and examined situations and learned custom. Then Lost Haven caught them in its little trap.

Were this a true Earth chronicle, there would be a buildup here. But Puca drama and life is otherwise. It has its own pace and climax, which is not that of Earth.

Something touches, something wilts, something dies. It is so told, and why should anything be added to it?

For now, in Lost Haven, Veronica had died suddenly, leaving the double family inconvenienced. She was the real head of the families, the mother of some of the children and the aunt of the rest of them. She had been their guarantee on Earth. No creature of any species could dislike her. That was not true of the rest of them.

She died of Earth Allergy, and all the adults of them suffered from it. "I can't very well die just yet," was the last thing she said. "Witchy is going out of her wits and she needs me. If I die, the family will break up." But it is no great thing for a Puca to die.

But Frank Dulanty took the death of his wife all wrong. Earth Sickness had tainted his viewpoint. His merriment at the wake was of a forced sort. The Bagarthach verses he made for it were funny, of course, but not really hilarious. He should have done much better.

The Puca believe, contrary to Earth people, that death is not an ending, but a mere passage to something new and interesting. Consequently, as do all who so believe, they make a happy celebration out of death.

But the Earth Allergy, attacking the liver and the kidneys (the seat of the good humor), taints one's views with the Earth outlook. It sours one on life. It even makes one, to a limited degree, fearful of death. It mixes a little wrong in all the right things.

"Henry, we can't live on this world," Frank said the next day.

"We were told to try," said Henry.

"We sicken, and now we die. It upsets all our plans. We are in danger of losing our patience and our balance, and of doing something that we may regret. And will the

20

children really be able to live here, Henry? Can they adapt to the world?''

''They have advantages,'' Henry said. ''They were born here, and, should already be immune to Earth Sickness. They have imagination and intelligence, and they can play Earth roles well.''

The two men watched the children from an upper window of the big shanty. The children were playing in the little choppy hills off to the southeast of Lost Haven, running and leaping out of trees and down hills. If they missed Veronica, they took it out with great activity and a sort of angry joy. And soon they were ravenous. Elizabeth glanced at the big shanty, and her father and uncle read her mind. It is a bother to go eat. One should eat on the run and the fly.

''Sing us a bird, Helen!'' Elizabeth called in a clear carrying voice, ''a big one with black juice in it!''

And Helen went into a sort of sly ecstasy and sang a Bagarthach verse towards the scuddy sky:

> *''I catch you, crow, in curving orb*
> *No matter how you caw and cough you!*
> *I sing the corbie to the corb!*
> *I sing the silly wings right off you!''*

Folks, there was a crow in the cloudy sky, and it jerked as though caught in a wire loop. It was dragged down through the steep air, cawing and coughing and fighting. Charles and Peter caught it as it came to their fingertips, and tore it to pieces with black gloss flying. They tore it apart and ate it up, gulping the black-red blood that tasted of hot salt and iron. You can have your white-meat barnyard peckers. This was their kind of bird.

Well, what Earth kid can sing a crow down from the

sky? Don't knock the trick till you can do it yourself.

"But no, Frank," Henry said as they watched their children from the distance. "They can't really adapt to Earth, I see it now. The question then becomes: Can the Earth adapt to them?"

Then Henry raised his head and listened as to the sounding of a horn off Earth.

3

High Purpose of the Gallant Band

If there were only six persons in the world (or seven, if you count Bad John), the Earth would be a much better place. All you had to do was kill all the other people on Earth. This, of course, must include not only the Earth people, but also the older Puca since they had the Earth Sickness.

The Elder Dulantys—and a handful of other Pucas on Earth—would have to be murdered with kindness and imagination. "Bam! I bet I'm good at killing people that way," Helen said, "I have so much of both." The older Dulantys were not happy here. And the children could, perhaps, have more fun when they were gone.

But this first step would be the ticklish one. You can't be killing your own parents and avunculi without having it worry you a little. After all, the children loved their parents with a blinding fury. But they had been raised to make intelligent decisions.

There was an easy answer to it. You can imagine that it's already done. Such a device would seem childish to Earth children, but Puca children have the means of putting their imagination into effect. They could sing a Bagarthach verse, and so make certain that it was done. They counted around by evens and odds, and it fell to Dorothy to sing the verse. She wasn't as good at them as

Helen or Peter, but it is the intention that counts in these things. Besides, it is nearly certain that Helen whispered one line to her. Dorothy sang the thing with a full dogged voice:

> *"We'll wither Witchy with a prank,*
> *And kindle them in flames like roses—*
> *Veronica and Hank and Frank—*
> *And give them all Apotheosis."*

So, the big shanty would burn down that very night, and everybody die in it except the six (or seven) children who would, fortunately, be out roistering around. The Bagarthach wasn't very well detailed, but these things work themselves out. Perhaps Papa Henry would have his throat slit by a blasted window pane in all that heat. Veronica was already dead, of course, but Dorothy forgot that part when she made up the verse. And the brains of Witchy, in a way, were already braised. "Hey, that works out pretty funny, that part about Mama," Helen said.

And after they were all roasted and put into their coffins, the rest of the road would be clear. You can't help it if your folks burn to death, especially if it's the best thing that could happen to them. And it would be the accomplishment of one of the great and valid dreams (even Earth children have it), to kill everyone in the world except your own small elite, and then to have the whole world cleared to do what you wanted with it.

They'd kill the Stutgards first, that very night, with axes. They'd axe old man Stutgard, and all the blood would run out of his big red neck. They'd cut off Mrs. Stutgard's head that was round as a pumpkin, and it would roll down to the bottom of the hill and look at you. They'd kill the Stutgard kids. It's most fun to kill kids who are just enough bigger than you to make it interesting.

Elizabeth, who was nine years old and already getting silly, at first had some doubts about killing everybody in the world. Kill the Stutgards and Crockers and Schermerhorns and Masters and Stones and Franklyns, sure. Especially Mr. Crocker who was the first man to bark at them when they came to Lost Haven. Kill Mrs. Cowper who had eyes like a little pig, and Mr. Kranker who had hairs in his ears. But Elizabeth thought that was enough to kill.

Her brother Charles partly supported her. He would, in addition, kill the Bacons and Lanyards and Kirbys, and possibly some of the Fabers. And Elwood Elgin and Rex Remagen and Barney Bottleby, three big boys, and Sheriff Train. But he thought that was almost enough.

So little Helen had to show them the big picture. The whole thing becomes silly unless you kill everybody, she said. And speaking about killing the older Dulantys, nine years old might be pretty near the borderline, she said, looking darkly at Elizabeth.

Peter and John were of Helen's way of thinking, and they bullied Dorothy into siding with them. They brought those older kids around and made it unanimous.

They'd start that very night. They'd kill Mr. Stutgard first of all. They drew straws for it, and John got the short straw.

The children went swimming in the bayou, to pass the afternoon till night should come and their big plan go into operation. You always do the first murders at night. Then, after you are onto the trick of them, you can do them in the daylight too.

They went swimming in the bayou, and they could swim! And they could dive like no children ever seen on

25

Earth before. Elizabeth who was the oldest was still the strongest swimmer, though little Helen was the fastest and slipperiest and hardest to catch. But it was Charles who dove from the highest branches, clear out of the very tops of the tall sycamores. And they could all stay under water as though it was their element.

Veronica had once told them that they must not stay under water too long at once. "If people are watching, they will wonder why you do not have to come up to breathe," she said.

But now Veronica was dead and gone and her advice unheeded. And somebody else was gone also, but in another way, and the children were still in a vague shock from it—the strangeness of such an un-Puca thing. A second disaster had struck the Dulantys the night before.

Now they swam and dived most of the afternoon. They frolicked in the three dimensions of the deep bayou, and seemed gay. Then they spread themselves out on the overhanging branches to dry off. Now they would have to think—but in parables, not directly.

A chicken will live for a little while after its head is cut off, and will not know what is the matter. And a young Dulanty will seem to survive mortal blows, with the action long delayed. But it *had* been another mortal blow, deprived even of the gaiety of death.

For Witchy had been taken away the night before. She had gone mad in a way that could not be ignored. We say not much about it yet. The shock has not taken its full effect. The second event, for the Pucas, was much the worse. But Veronica and Witchy were both lost to the families now. Earth Sickness was stifling the family. Could they live on this world any longer?

Four of the children told fanciful stories as they dried

out on the branches and waited for the night. They were parables of things not to be admitted directly. *But three of the stories had already happened*, and the prophetic story of little Helen would happen that very night.

"There was this little girl," said Elizabeth, "and her mother went out of the shanty one night. It got later and her mother didn't come back, so at midnight the little girl put on her dress and went to look for her.

"She went down the dark streets where the houses were hid in the weeds and the trees leaned together and touched each other across the street. The little girl could smell her mother's perfume the way she had gone. Then the girl saw a crazy floozy up ahead making a crazy noise.

"So Elizabeth went up to the floozy (no she didn't, her name wasn't Elizabeth. I don't know what it was)—so the little girl went up to the floozy to ask her if she had seen her mother. But the floozy screamed and ran down a dark street.

"And Elizabeth—I mean the little girl—ran down the street after her till it came to a place where it closed in and the floozy couldn't run any further; and people were stumbling out of their houses to see what the screaming was all about. Then the floozy turned around, and the light from somewhere fell on her face.

" 'My God, Elizabeth!' the floozy said. No she didn't—she said, 'My God'—whatever the little girl's name was—'that you should see me like this.' Then the little girl screamed too, because the floozy had eyes just like her mother's; only they were cracked and her face was crooked. And Elizabeth didn't know whether it was her mother or not, but she thought *it had been* her mother.

"It was a crazy Earth-people face that the floozy had. How could a Puca face be crazy? It was like a mask turned into a face, and the real face melted away behind it. Dying

27

is fun, or everybody makes out that it's fun. Going crazy is *not* fun, and nobody can make it so.

"Then the people had to tie that floozy up like a dog and take her to the hospital.

"The little girl ran all the way home and climbed up and looked into the looking-glass over the sink in the kitchen. Would you believe it? It wasn't her at all. She laughed, she was so relieved. Then she looked around, and it wasn't even her own house she was in. It had all happened to somebody else and to somebody else's mother."

Elizabeth had the blackest hair and the whitest skin in the world, but now her skin shivered. She lay stretched out on an old branch up against the sky, a live image too real to be real.

Now they were all one quarter dry from their swim.

"There was this little boy," said Peter, "and he sat in the kitchen and watched his father one night. His father had a brown bottle and a glass. His father winked at him, but there was something just a little bit wrong with that wink. Then his father poured the glass full and drank it. It made his father look a little more like an Earth man. The father began to change when he drank it, like the man in the story that changed into a frog when he drank the drops off a mushroom. Then the father winked again, but his face was still differenter when he did it; and he drank another glass.

"The third time he did it, when he winked again and when he opened his eyes after the wink, there wasn't any eye there, just a gray glaze. The father kept changing, his face got redder and his arms got darker. He winked with his other eye; and when he opened it, the other eye was gone too. He drank the whole blamed bottle empty.

"Then the man got littler and littler like a frog. 'I bet

there's still a little bit in the corner of the bottle if I could get to it,' the man said. Then he crawled inside the bottle and found another good drink down in the very corner of it. No he didn't. I just made that part up. He didn't get any littler, and he didn't crawl into the bottle. It was just a notion the little boy had that his father was about to do.

"Then the man broke the empty bottle on the edge of the table, and put his head down in the middle of the broken glass and went to sleep. Then Peter—then the little boy, not Peter—watched the man all night. But when the sun shined in the window in the morning, Peter saw that it was a different man, not his father. He didn't know what had happened to his father. He is afraid to see if his own father has come back yet today."

They were half dry from their swim now. It was near evening.

"There was this other little boy," said John, "and his mother. All they had to eat was one onion. Every night they ate one layer of it till it was all gone. Then the mother lay down and died, but the little boy didn't know she was dead. It was the first time he had run into a situation like this. The little boy went out and stole another onion and brought it to her. But there were some more people in the house then, and they had put his mother into a crate.

" 'Your mother is dead,' they told him, and he was both glad and sorry to hear it. 'I'll give her the onion anyhow,' he said. 'They keep you from getting colds, and I think she has to cross a wet river to get where she's going.' He put it in her hand, but she gripped the little boy's hand in hers, and it was like cold iron. 'Let me go,' he said, but she was dead and couldn't hear him, and she gripped him all the harder. There wasn't any way to get him loose from her. 'Well, we don't have all day to waste,' one of the men said, 'somebody get a bone saw and let's cut this little boy's arm off.' 'Judas priest! Don't do that to me,' the little boy said. 'Wherever I go, I want it to be all of me.' 'Well, get in or get out,' the men told him. The little boy couldn't make up his mind, so the men pushed him down into the crate and nailed down the lid, and buried him there with his mother. It scared him to death to be buried like that.''

Now they were all three-quarters dry from their swim. The children had believed they were poor because they were living in the big shanty. They thought that Veronica had starved to death, though the house was always full of food. Elizabeth had recently read a story about a woman who had starved to death, and she had embellished the story to the rest of them, and it was on their minds.

''There was a little girl and they put her father in jail,'' Helen said. ''It was the sheriff that did it. The little girl went to see her father in jail, but they wouldn't let her in to see him. 'You go home and forget about him,' those men told her, 'he's so far back in there that we have to shoot his beans to him.' 'I thought that was just a joke they made up about people in jail,' Helen said. 'Not this time,' they told her, 'we've got him so deep in the cooler that we couldn't get him out with an ice-pick.' 'I thought that was just a blamed way of talking,' Helen said. 'Not this time,' the men told her, 'we got him so far in there that we got to pipe sunshine to him.' 'I thought that was a blasted colloquialism,' the little girl said. 'Naw, we locked him up and throwed away the key,' they told her. 'Won't the key show up as short on inventory control?' the little girl asked. 'I'll fix you guys,' the little girl said, so she sang a Bagarthach verse:

> *" 'I blast you corny country cops,*
> *I'll blow the bars and locks, by hokey!*
> *I'll kill the sheriff's cows and crops,*
> *And get my papa out of pokey.'*

"Say, that Bagarthach verse didn't work at all. It didn't blow the bars and locks or do a thing to that jail. You know the reason? It was all a dream. Lots of times a Bagarthach won't work in a dream. None of it had really happened to the girl and her father, not yet at least.

"But the girl knew that she would never see her father any more, so she stole a boat and went to sea to be a sailor. I forget whether this was while she was dreaming or after she woke up."

"How'd she know which way to go?" Dorothy asked.

"She went down Mud Bayou till it runs into Crow Creek in the strip pits," Helen told her. "She went down Crow Creek till it goes into Green River, down Green River till it goes into the Arkansas River, down the Arkansas till it goes into the Mississippi, and down the Mississippi till it goes in the Ocean. It's downhill all the way and you can't miss it."

By this time they were completely dry, so they put on their clothes and gave the trees back to the sulky crows who were returning from the fields. They went to hide in Stutgard's fruit cellar till it was dark enough for John to kill Mr. Stutgard.

Bad John was their lookout, for he could be outside the cellar, and then inside again, or into the Stutgards' house and in all the rooms of it, and out again without using the doors or without anyone seeing him. But he wasn't a very good lookout. He couldn't tell them whether it was dark yet or not. He didn't know what it meant to be dark.

But just when Helen had looked out and told them that it

was dark enough, Bad John came back to them. He told them that it was no good anyhow, that John could not kill Mr. Stutgard.

"Why can't I kill him?" John demanded. "Here I am almost four foot tall and as salty a man or boy as there is on Earth. I can kill anybody I want to."

But a man had already killed Mr. Stutgard, and he was dead, Bad John told them.

"What man?" Peter demanded. "Nobody better be poaching on our preserve. We thought of it to kill him first."

Bad John told them what man had killed Mr. Stutgard.

"Why, you are just silly," Helen told Bad John. "He would be the last one in the world to kill him. I think we better get a dog to be our lookout man the next time we kill somebody at night."

They didn't believe Bad John, and they went about it to do it themselves. The children came under the window of the high room where Mr. Stutgard spent his evenings. John had his small axe ready, and as sharp as a corn knife.

Peter stood on Elizabeth's shoulders, and Helen on Peter's, and Dorothy on Helen's, and Charles on Dorothy's. Then John climbed up the swaying tower of them with his axe in his hand. He went in through the window which Bad John had left unlatched. Bad John could do things like that, as he could work from either the inside or the outside of a room.

John was in there quite a while. The swaying tower of children chittered in anticipation like a grove full of crickets.

John came out with the bloody dripping axe in his hands, and climbed down them, and then they climbed down each other. Then they all ran away, for a sudden great screaming was heard from the Stutgard house.

They reassembled in a dark lane full of pigweeds and sunflowers.

"You did it! You did it!" the happy children screamed.

"No, I didn't do it," said John sadly and with a frustration older than his six years.

"But you did! You did!" exulted Helen. "Just feel all the nice blood on the axe. People who don't love blood don't love anything."

"No," John said. "Bad John was right. Mr. Stutgard was already killed. That man got him before I could."

"Just imagine a man killing another man, and neither of them a Puca," Elizabeth shuddered. "It almost makes me sick. But how did you get all that blood on your axe then?"

But they all saw at once that it was not the little boy's axe that John held now. It was a heavy man's axe, nine times as big as John's little one. And it was covered with blood.

"It hasn't started the way I intended it," Helen said. So they all started home in the dark, still excited over the murder that they had come so close to doing.

It was when they came near where the old shanty used to be that they saw something that really astonished them. They had to look twice, and then they hardly believed it. It loomed up in the dark as it did every night, and their fathers were inside under the lights.

The big shanty was still there! It had not burned down at all. Their Bagarthach verse had somehow failed in its effect. Well, it was something that would have to be lived with.

Tomorrow they'd make a better Bagarthach, comical and correct, that would kill Henry and Frank Dulanty correctly. And it was good to sleep one more night under the same roof with them.

They left the bloody axe on the back porch, and all went up to bed.

4

And Six Were Kids, and One a Ghostie

It was a little after midnight that six men (they were Sheriff Train and five hasty deputies) came with flashlights and rifles to arrest Henry Dulanty for the murder of Coalfactor Stutgard.

"He is dead?" asked Henry. "—A silly question if I am to be taken for his murder. But you all know that I couldn't have done it."

"We don't know anything about you or what you could do," said the sheriff. "You have several times threatened his life."

"I have never done anything so trivial," said Henry.

"At least there have been angry words between the two of you, which amounts to the same thing when testimony is given," said the sheriff. "For your own safety, I am going to have you lodged in the county jail. The Lost Haven jail wouldn't keep you in if you decided to get out, I know; and it wouldn't keep the men out if they decided to go in after you. It's no more than a crackerbox. You aren't liked by the people here, you know. They say that you are neither fish nor flesh."

"Must I be one or the other?" Henry asked. "Oh well, I'll go with you after a bit then; but first I must talk with my brother here alone, and then take care of a few other things.''

"You're not going to talk to anybody alone. If you're going to say anything, say it real fast right now, and then come along,'' Sheriff Train ground out, and he looked around to his five green deputies for support.

"Frank,'' Henry said, "put the bottle away. You have to look after the children now. This is three of us they lost in three days: one dead, one demented, one arrested with intent to lynch. Now they have only yourself.''

(Since the death of his wife Veronica two days before, Frank Dulanty had been drinking in a blind stupor. It was a Specific against Earth Allergy, he said. His despondency had been deepened by the derangement of his brother's wife Witchy.)

"I'll put it away,'' Frank said, "and I'll take care of the children if they seem to need care, a thing hard to imagine. I will also do what can be done about this other thing. But you don't have to go unless you want to, Henry. You're not sick enough to believe that you have to go with them. I will settle these six quaking lawmen and their hardware if you wish, or you can do it yourself. Neither of us have fallen so low that six of their sort could give us trouble.''

"But this is their hour,'' said Henry, "and the power of darkness.''

"What kind of talk is that?'' Sheriff Train demanded.

"From Luke,'' said Henry. "He was an Earth writer, but he could almost have made it as a Puca.''

The men led big Henry Dulanty away then—like a confused bull with a new ring in his nose. They would never have ringed him had he not been shot through with Earth Allergy and its accompanying listlessness. Nevertheless, they were six shaking men with their rifles, and he was calm.

Well, did *you* ever arrest a goblin or ogre who stood six feet four and was as heavy as a yearling ox? One who, it was said, could rot the flesh off your bones by making a rime about you?

But they took him away. Then Frank and the children went to bed with a chill on their spirits. They all slept till morning, except Elizabeth. She arose, as soon as the house was quiet, and went out on the porch and got the bloody axe and hid it.

"I think you children should stay very close to the house till we see what is going to happen," Frank said the next morning.

"I think we should do no such thing," said little Helen, "and I know what will happen. A welfare lady will come and take us away. They'll put us in a home, and we'll get stubborn and we won't eat, and we'll all be dead within a week. I think that we'd better be hard to find. And—ah—I guess we won't have you killed for a while yet. You're the only one of the parents left, and we might need you. We sent a Bagarthach to get you all yesterday, but something went wrong with it."

"We shot your Bagarthach down with another one," Frank said. "You can't use them against the Kindred. And, kids, don't ever kill Pucas! Nor even Earth people unless you have a good reason for it. I thought we'd told you that before. Yes, possibly it is best that you be hard to find. I don't believe anybody can find you if you don't want to be found. I will go see Witchy today, and Henry in jail, and get a lawyer, and find what friends I can. I'll be back tonight, though. If you don't come back, then send someone to tell me that you're all right."

The children went out into the town and considered it.

"It is time that we became persons in this world," Charles said. "We need a base of operations, a moving one."

"Come along then," Helen said.

The children went to the little tin jail of Lost Haven to talk to Fulbert Fronsac. This was not, of course, like the strong jail at the county seat where their father-uncle Henry was held. This was a flimsy little jail that seldom had more than one prisoner, who was in residence now. The children entered the little jail by the hole in the roof, as they always did.

"Misere!" said Fulbert, the prisoner, when he saw them. "That tragedy should strike you again! There are days when the Good God is not good. He and I are due a serious talk on this very matter today. Ah, you have brought *Ange-Jacques* with you!

Fulbert was one of the few regular people who could see Bad John, and he called him *Ange-Jacques.* Fulbert was an old French bum who was also the lost Dauphin. And, if not he, then he was the son of the Dauphin, or the grandson, sometimes the one, sometimes the other. But to the town, he was the town drunk.

The Puca (the same as with Indians) were always in rapport with French drunks. And the trouble (again in this case) was just that there weren't enough French drunks in this part of the country.

Fulbert, however, was a man of property. He owned both the *Ile de France* and Catherine de Medici. The *Ile* was a fishing raft that Fulbert used on the streams and canals of the strip pits, and on Crow Creek and Green River.

Catherine de Medici was a she-goat who (like Fulbert) was of royal blood. She was the great-great-granddaughter of the first Catherine de Medici, the queen of

France. How it happened that, being so, she was a goat and not a person, is another story.

"There must be an end to this *idiotie*," Fulbert said. "I know that your loving father-uncle would not kill a man. He could and has flattened noses and scattered his share of teeth in his short time here. He hasn't made himself popular with the people of Lost Haven. All are afraid of him, and he the kindest of men! But he did not kill that man."

"No, he couldn't have killed Mr. Stutgard," Dorothy said. "He was already dead."

"Who was already dead, my favorite goblin?" Fulbert asked her.

"I don't know anything about goblins, but Mr. Stutgard was already dead when we went to kill him. Bad John was watching them when the man killed him, and it wasn't Uncle Henry."

"Who did kill Mr. Stutgard, kids?" Fulbert asked them.

So they told Fulbert who had killed Mr. Stutgard. And they gave him all the details. And Fulbert thought about it quite a while before he spoke.

"It isn't very tangible evidence," Fulbert said, "mostly because *Ange-Jacques* isn't a very tangible boy. Do any of you know what time it was when you were in the fruit cellar? Had any of you a watch?

"No," John said, "but Helen knows how to tell time if we had one."

"*Ange-Jacques* could not testify in court," Fulbert mused. "There are advantages as well as disadvantages to invisibility. And invisibility combined with inaudibility is a combination hard to touch."

"We could tell people what Bad John told us," Peter said. "And if they ask a question, we can ask him for them. When he answers, we can tell them the answer. A lot of people can't hear him talk, you know.''

''I know,'' Fulbert said. ''People being constituted as they are, it wouldn't be too successful. But this isn't why you came to see me today.''

''No,'' Helen told him. ''Charles said that we needed a moveable base of operations. And I, being the most intelligent of us, immediately comprehended what it should be.''

''She means,'' Elizabeth explained to Fulbert, ''that we came to get a deed from you to the *Ile de France*. We need it in our business, and we don't want to steal it from you without a deed.''

''A deed wouldn't be binding unless you gave me a consideration,'' Fulbert told them. ''Give me a dollar to make it legal. The timber alone is worth a dollar, not counting the craftsmanship. If you haven't a dollar, then go steal me a bottle of whisky. Or have you scruples about stealing whisky without a deed to it?''

''Helen's the only one that knows what scruples are and she won't tell us,'' John said. ''Have we scruples about it, Helen?''

''Not a trace,'' Helen affirmed. ''And I know just where there is one. I'll take John with me and make him get it. We're trying to get him over being so bashful about going into people's houses and stealing things. Come along, John, we have to be back before these children manage to mess up the whole deal.''

''Let's write the deed right now before she gets back,'' Elizabeth said. ''Hurry. You've no idea how much time it saves to do things when she's gone.''

''I'll write it.'' Peter said. ''It'll look better in a man's hand. Besides, I'm not sure whether the Salic Law obtains in Crow Creek Township."

"Oh, you talk just like Helen!" said Elizabeth.

"Has anybody a paper and pencil?" Peter asked. "You scratch out a deed on a shingle with a nail and somebody's going to look down on it."

"I have them," said Fulbert, producing the objects. "In my youth I was a natural son of Le Franc de Pompignan, and I always carry writing materials in case I should be taken suddenly with an ode."

"To whomever it is respected," Peter wrote slowly in a solemn voice after taking the paper and pencil. "This is to convey one raft the Ile de France with the boathouse and blanket and lantern and automobile horn and the box of snuff and the frying pan and the coffee pot and other accessories in fee simple for one bottle of whiskey stolen by Helen and John Dulanty and given in token to Fulbert Fronsac, dated today (I don't know the date and I bet nobody else does either) and agreeable to all parties."

It took him a long time to get this out, speaking a word at a time as he wrote it.

"Put down 'Witnessed and amended by all parties present,' " Charles said.

"All right. Whoops! Finished just in time. She's back!" Peter completed the document.

"You forgot what to do about Catherine de Medici," Helen chortled as she returned with John and the stolen whisky. "I knew, of course, that you would go ahead on your own the moment my back was turned. I knew also that you would botch it. Just let me see it a minute. Not as bad as I feared. Fortunately there is nothing here that a thoughtful person can't quickly put to rights. Catherine is a sea goat, not a land goat. She lives on the *Ile* most of the time."

"We will put in a clause that she can be our guest for as

long as she likes," Charles suggested. "And we will let her off at any port if she wants to visit friends or has business to transact."

"How long will you be using the *Ile?* Fulbert asked them.

"For as long as we like," Peter said. "You see, we're going to kill everybody in the world, and that includes you. You won't be needing the raft any more after that so we're doing you a favor buying it from you. Please sign this (Helen's written in the new clauses), and then we will all sign."

They all signed. Bad John could not write the way others wrote, but he used a different kind of pencil and made a queer mark. Fulbert was near frightened when he saw it, and he muttered something in a tongue older than French.

There was this else about the mark that Bad John made. When, later that week, the children showed the deed to a certain lawyer and to others, none of those people could see Bad John's mark though it was plain as the face on your head.

After this, the children went to the boat raft, checked it over carefully in maritime terms, provisioned it and set sail to be gone forever.

5

A Child's a Monster Still Uncurled

The strip pits are a dozen square miles of mountains turned inside out, threaded by canals, and with bottomless chasms. The artificial hills are full of shafts and pits and caves both above and below water level. Coalfactor Stutgard owned all this, but he had closed down the coal mines several years before.

The Dulanty children loved the pits. Their own home world (which they had never seen) was made up of land and water inextricably mixed, with endless caves inside the hills, and even better caves below the water level. These old waterlogged surface coal pits made a good substitute, and they'd claim every watery acre of the pits as soon as they got the *Ile* to moving properly.

Fulbert had told the children that Catherine de Medici knew how the small sail on the *Ile de France* should be rigged, in case they could not figure it out for themselves. There was something they meant to ask him about that but they forgot. That old bat Fulbert had twinkled his eye when he said it, and he was a tricky one.

Of course Catherine knew how the sail should be rigged. She had seen it done hundreds of times. But, being a goat, she could neither do it herself nor tell them how it should be done. Finally, Charles figured it out.

There were five kingdoms in the strip pits that the children had to reduce before they went on to exterminate the people of the rest of the world. You can't leave unreduced strongholds behind you when you go into the exterminating business.

First of the five kingdoms was that of the Stinkers, a club composed of Elwood Elgin, Rex Remagen, and Berny Bottleby—three big boys, the oldest of them eleven years old.

The *Ile de France* billowed boldly up to Port Stinker with Helen laboring the old automobile horn for a warning and a challenge. The Stinkers came out to do battle in their own craft, the *Sea Bear*.

"You look like pigs and you're not people at all," Elwood Elgin challenged them.

"You hop like frogs and you eat raw fish," Rex Remagen sang out.

"You swim like pollywogs and you got tails like them," Berny Bottleby shouted.

It's the half-truths that kill you. Only three of the Dulantys looked like goblins, which is *not* the same thing as looking like pigs—except under the eyes where the snoot begins, and where the ears fasten on. They did *not* hop like frogs, though they could leap further and higher than regular people could. Sure, they ate catfish raw, but sometimes they fried or baked other fish if they had time for it. Of course they swam like pollywogs; it's easier to slither your whole body than just to churn your arms and legs. And they did *not* have tails, none that amounted to anything.

That was war talk the Stinkers were hollering at them, so let it be war then! Helen let go with a Bagarthach verse that should have settled the Stinkers forever:

"Oh Stinker limbs that reek and rot,
A Stinker head that decomposes!
We'll splatter all the blood you've got,
You seven-letter sos-and-soses!"

The two vessels moved towards each other at a combined speed of more than three miles an hour. But the *Sea Bear* had forgotten to mount any artillery, while Charles and John both had a great store of throwing rocks. And Elizabeth had mighty cannon-crackers that she lighted and tossed.

But it was Helen, with a variant of Greek fire, who broke the Stinkers' center. These were paper sacks which she set afire and flung with rock warheads to give them carrying power. They landed and flamed on the deck of the *Sea Bear* as the battling craft came close. The hardy Stinkers attempted to stamp them out barefooted, and that was where the battle turned against them. The Stinkers suddenly began to holler and carry on like crazy.

The burning sacks were filled with splinters of glass, thumbtacks, cockleburs, cactus, and devil-claws, all imbedded in a soft matrix. You stamp down on those barefooted and you're hurt. The Stinkers were wounded, and the deck of the *Sea Bear* was red with their blood.

Yet this was only a diversion, not the main attack. The Dulantys knew, even if the Stinkers had temporarily forgotten, that inside the Stinker shack was a .22 rifle. Now Peter made his move. He slipped over the far side of the *Ile de France,* swam under both craft, and made shore. He was inside the Stinker stockade, had the .22, and was out barking orders:

"Hold, halt, stand, abaft!"

"You don't even know how to shoot it!" Rex Remagen yipped savagely, deep in his own pain.

45

But Peter did know how to shoot it. He shot it, "Ka-zing!" And then there was silence.

"Now, if one of you will just put that boy's ear back on, we will get down to business," Peter said.

The *Sea Bear,* in the meantime, had been boarded by the Dulantys. Elizabeth, never one to miss a turn like that, came up behind the stunned Stinkers and slapped a handful of fish innards from a bait bucket to the side of each Stinker head. Each thought that it was himself who had lost an ear and that it had been replaced.

"Truss the prisoners," ordered Peter, one of the most astute eight-year-old generals in the world. The Stinkers were bound up, and a rock tied around the neck of each. Elizabeth hit each of them sharply on the head with a pipe wrench, and Charles and John booted them off the craft to their destruction.

"Death and destruction!" Helen sang. "See all the nice bloody water." And the Dulantys began to jubilate, and let their guard down.

For, possibly because of faulty staff work, the spot of execution was near water only two feet deep. This was the Stinkers' own water, and they knew the shallows. They swarmed onto shore, for only their arms had been tied, and disappeared around a shoulder of rock.

Following them on shore, after a stunned interval, was no good. Kids always know their own stronghold, and the Stinkers knew theirs. They had escaped.

"It's a black failure," said Charles. "I hold myself partly responsible. Let us consider our strategy so that a thing like this can never happen again."

"It is no great matter," Helen said. "What I really want is for you little children to learn tactics, and you learn by your failures. They won't live long. I put chicken dirt and cow dirt and dog dirt and people dirt in my fire bombs.

If they don't die of their head wounds, the lockjaw will kill them by sundown."

The Dulantys burned down the Stinker shack and cursed anyone who should assemble there again. The Dulanty navy had now been doubled by the capture of the *Sea Bear*, and the Dulantys had a weapon in the .22. They had reduced one of the strongholds of the strip-pit country.

The screen and canvas shack of the Stutgard children, the second kingdom of the pits, seemed to be deserted. But it was heavy, and it could be moved but slightly on its piers of rock-filled oil drums. The Dulantys started a bonfire under its floor to kindle the old crib. They got it to burning pretty good.

But the shack hadn't been empty. As the fires arose, Amada Stutgard jumped out of the building and ran back into the hills. And Peter started after her.

"Mind you, no mercy," Helen called after him. "You are instructed to bring back her ears as proof that you've killed her."

"All right," Peter called back, but he was worried as he ran. He didn't have a knife or anything else to cut her ears off with. By the time Peter had caught her and thrown her down on the ground, they were out of sight of the others. He pinned her down, kneeling on her. She was a big girl, ten years old.

"Where were you?" Peter demanded.

"I have a place up in the rafters where I hide when I want to cry," she gasped. She went up and down with her breath as he knelt on her stomach. It was like riding in a boat. "I was crying because my father is dead," she whimpered.

"Why'd you cry for that? He was the meanest man in the country. Do you know what I'm going to do to you,

Amada? I'm going to push you down in the quicksand and stand on you till you go down, and jump off your face at the last minute, and you'll die with your mouth full of green mud.''

"The quicksand's half a mile from here.''

"Let's get started then. I don't want to lose time.''

"All right,'' Amada said queerly. She was half again as big as Peter, but he gripped her soft wrists so as almost to sever her hands from her arms.

"Why don't you let me go, Peter?'' Amada said when they were halfway to the quicksand. "Nobody would have to know.''

"I can't. I have to cut off your ears and bring them back to Helen to prove that I killed you.''

"Why don't you break a couple of pods off one of those Cherokee creepers and bring them to her? They're ear-colored.''

"I couldn't do that. You wouldn't want me to cheat, would you?''

They came quickly to the quicksand.

"This is as good a spot as any,'' Peter said.

"Let me get that clump of grass across the draw,'' Amada said. "I'll spread it out to lie down on the quicksand on.''

"You give your word to come back?''

"I give my word.''

"All right. And see if you can find a real sharp rock over there to cut off your ears with. These here aren't very good.''

Then Amada went away. But she crossed the little draw and was up a hill like a swooping lark, running so fast that Peter wondered what was the matter with her. Then he understood. She was very near her own house, and Peter wouldn't be able to catch her.

"Your uncle killed my father," she cried fiercely when she was safe. "And you are dirty and ugly and you look like a porky-pine."

Peter was shaken by the deception. He learned that Earth people will lie to save their lives and will say a thing when they don't mean it. Earth people are the most treacherous creatures in all the universes.

But that didn't get Peter past Helen. There was only one thing to do. He broke a couple of the flesh-colored pods off a Cherokee creeper and handed them carelessly to Helen as the ears of Amada Stutgard, as soon as he got back.

Helen exploded, and Peter's heart sank; he should have known that she was too smart to accept them. But her fury wasn't turned onto Peter.

"Kids, we don't know what we got ahold of!" she screeched. "I swear these ears are partly, at least, vegetable fiber. What *are* Earth people, anyhow? What ungodly half-plant half-animals have we got ourselves involved with? And look, there's seeds inside the ears like a pod. Earth-people seeds! Do you suppose that's the way they generate? Kill them all as fast as we can, I say! They're monsters!"

They plowed up Stutgard Landing and sowed it with salt. Or at least they made a symbolic scratch, and shook salt into it. And no grass ever grew there again. No grass had ever grown on that sour mud flat before.

The next objective, the kingdom of the Fiddlers, was hard to find. The Fiddlers made illegal whisky, and their place was the best hidden in the pits. The sheriff had never been able to find it. But Catherine de Medici knew the way, and she showed the direction by her attitude. They came to Fiddler's Landing—it was only a gash in the hills where one could nose a boat. Helen sounded the automobile horn for a challenge.

Jack Fiddler was a suspicious man. He stuck his head out from behind an unlikely hill, and he had them covered with a blunderbuss before they saw him.

"Ha! Ye've stolen the *Ile* from old Fulbert!" Jack Fiddler intoned at them. "Have you killed the vicious old saint, ye evil kindred?"

"No, we're going to leave him till one of the last," Peter explained reasonably. "We've come to kill you now. Boy, I bet we blast you wide open."

"I'll just come aboard and belabor the crowd of you and get to the truth about this raft stealing," Jack Fiddler growled. And that is where he made his mistake.

When Jack Fiddler bounded aboard the raft, he left his rifle leaning against a rock on shore. And when he collared the first two children to bounce their heads together, he found himself looking down the small but serious barrel of the .22 into the weird green eyes of Peter.

That Jack Fiddler carried on like a crazy man when they had the jump on him. He roared and pawed the plank decking, but he couldn't scare the boy loose from the weapon. Then Fiddler folded, swallowed his cud, as they say. They ordered him around, and he went meekly, but with an evil sly look in his eye and a bide-my-time set to his mouth. But Charles had Fiddler's big rifle now, and there was nothing the man could do.

They made him get a wheelbarrow and rig a plank and load a barrel of corn whisky and a barrel of choc beer and a tubful of mash. The mash smelled as good and as sour as anything you ever nosed.

"It will be good to eat for breakfast," Dorothy said.

They made Fiddler load a ham that his last customer had just left with him. Then they told him to kneel down in the mud and say his prayers, that his time had come to die.

But Jack Fiddler did no such thing. He bounded off into his tricky rocks and hills, whipping and evading like a cotton-tail going to ground, as the .22 and the big rifle barked in futile pursuit of him. That Jack Fiddler had been shot at more than once before, that was clear. They weren't about to get him.

The Dulanty kids would have to do something about letting their jumped prey escape them every time. Oh well, they could send a Bagarthach verse after him to kill him. And there was plenty to do wrecking his stuff.

They turned over the rest of his barrels, sank his boat, and set fire to his wagon. But they couldn't find his house to burn it. The sheriff had never been able to find it either, or his main reserve stock for that matter.

Now the Dulantys had a second rifle much larger than the .22. And they had corn whisky and beer instead of rum. Helen, who was on a pirate jag lately, had wished for rum.

But the whisky and choc would serve as well, for fashions change in both piracy and liquor.

6

The World's a Trap, and None Can Quit It—

The next objective of the Dulantys was the stronghold of the Lanyard family, but here they ran into difficulties that were mostly mental. It is hard to plunder a people who will willingly give you anything they have. The Lanyards were good people, and they did not themselves know how many were in their family. It depends on where you start and finish counting.

The Lanyards were part Shawnee Indian, which made them better than the Fiddlers, who were part Quapaw, and better than the Fabers who were part Cherokee.

Well, it had to be done nevertheless. You can't start getting kind to people when there's a job to do. The Dulantys landed to a terrific blast of the old automobile horn and the terrible cry of Peter:

"A swift and merciful death is the best we can offer. Don't make us do our worst."

The Lanyards were either off somewhere, or else they were too terrified to show a head. Finally there appeared Phoebe Jane Lanyard, the mother of the brood, in answer to the racket. She came out openly, and did not seem to comprehend her danger.

Phoebe had always had a way of looking at the Dulantys and chuckling, without answering their extravagances.

She understood this goblin brood better than anyone else did, and she mocked their own look back at them with a rakish looseness of features. She could be as goblin as they could.

The goblin look, as you know, is characterized by an extreme mobility of the features. "We can look like regular people till we have to laugh," Peter had said once. Even the non-goblin-appearing of the Dulantys (the beautiful Elizabeth and Charles and Helen) had increasingly taken on the goblin hue these last several days. "Look at them sideways and they're goblins too," Phoebe Jane said out loud—to herself, not to them. She had a talent for looking at things sideways.

Phoebe's chuckling at all their threats got the Dulantys' goat, and we don't mean Catherine de Medici. They stormed onto shore and blazed at her with green eyes that they tried to make angry.

"You do well to hide out in the pits," she said to them, seriously now, when they were on shore. "They are having a meeting on you today, and there will be an order to put you in a home. Crocker is behind it."

"We hate him!" Elizabeth spat. "We really ought to go back and kill him before we kill you."

"I think so too," Phoebe said. "I'd appreciate it if you'd leave me pretty well to the last."

Phoebe Jane was more Indian than the rest of her family, for her husband was a good part white. Sometimes Phoebe said that she was Shawnee and French and that Jean Chouteau was her grandfather; or that she was Shawnee and Texas and Charles Goodnight was her grandfather; or Shawnee and Arkansas and Jessie Chisholm was her grandfather; or Shawnee and Missouri and both Jessie and Frank James were her grandfathers. She was also granddaughter of Charles Curtis, Chief Crazy Horse,

David Payne, and Sequoyah. The reason she had so many grandfathers was that she came from a big family.

And by now she had surveyed everything on board both of the rafts.

"I think that a group in your position should be willing to barter," she told them. "I will just take that keg of corn whisky—my husband and children love it so much. Here, here, give a hand, kids. You'll get back full value."

She wheeled the keg of corn off the *Ile* on a little loop-wheeled cart, set it up on chocks with the help of Charles and Peter, and broached it to see if it was good. It was. She liked it.

Then she brought to the Dulantys a big gunny sack of pecans, a jug of grape juice that was just beginning to turn heady, some jars of hominy, and a slab of deer meat as hard and black as old leather.

"Now you kids be gone before someone comes," she said. "They know you come here often, and they're looking for you. Stay hidden in some inlet for the rest of today and tonight and tomorrow. I'll find you tomorrow night and tell you what has happened to Henry and Frank, whether they have hung either of them yet. I'll see Witchy the next day. I'd try to get permission to keep you kids with me but they wouldn't allow it, me being only a common-law wife and having seven children and three grandchildren and quite a few other people all living in one shack. But I am the one you are to look to while you are hiding out in the pits."

"How will you find us tomorrow night, as slick as we can hide, and when we don't even know where we're going to be?" John asked.

"I will find you," Phoebe said. "Now go quickly. I know when people are going to come to my place, and people will be here very soon."

The *Ile* and the *Sea Bear* weighed anchor, or anyhow were poled away from the bank by the Dulanty crew.

"*A-wa-wa-shingay!*" all the Dulantys called to Phoebe as they left. It was all the Shawnee words they knew.

"*A-wa-way*," Phoebe called softly after them.

"We *got* to start killing people," Charles said. "We can't keep leaving everybody till last."

But at the final principality in the strip pits there could be no question of mercy. This was the stronghold of the Fabers. From past raids, the Fabers hated the Dulanty children with a white hatred, and the Dulantys hated the Fabers. But this would be a dangerous sortie. The Fabers were commercial fisherman and they knew every splash of water in their region. Besides, as was common talk among children both Puca and Earthian, the Fabers weren't above killing a stray child who came their way and chopping him up for bait. There wasn't any real evidence for this, some of those damned cooler heads used to say. Of course there wasn't! What can you do when the evidence is already used up for bait? Who else catches so many fish as the Fabers? It has to be the kind of bait they are using that makes the difference.

The Dulanty armada stalked in quietly, splashless and furtive. It hid itself till two rowboats with two fishermen in each passed them going down to Green River to run and rebait their trotlines. The Faber day-fishers had not yet come up Crow Creek that evening.

The Dulantys eased into Faber Landing where there was only one boat, and that one did not seem to be in recent use. Well, there was the stronghold before them, the shack, the privy, the open-front boathouse, the net racks, the bait tubs. Where was the strategic point to strike?

Charles and Peter fired a number of shots through the Faber privy. The .22 pitted pleasantly into the wood, and the .30 seemed to tear through the front of it and embed its shots in the back boards. The privy made a nice little echo box, almost like a drum.

"If there's anybody in there, he's sure dead now," Peter said. So they tried the shack from their distance. They fired a dozen shots through the door of the shack and got no answer. Now was the time for frontal assault.

"Hit the beach!" Peter howled. "Land ho!"

"What's so funny about land?" Dorothy asked.

They hit the shack in a wave of small flesh. Bad John went through and unlatched the door for them from the inside. Nobody was there. They broke out the shack window, and started a good fire inside the building. They threw furniture on, and cord and cloth, and some shoemakers' wax to make it smell good; the Fabers apparently employed this somehow in their net-lashing. Then the fire took the whole shack so fast that the children had to scurry to get out. It was the fastest and best fire they ever started.

Then they got to it. They dumped several hundred pounds of good fish from the tanks into the pit streams. They armed themselves with fish knives and discovered that these were just what they had been needing all their lives. They slashed nets and gear, and piled and burned everything that would burn. They loaded two one-hundred-hook trotlines onto the *Sea Bear* where they would be handy. They took the last and best tray of bait, and a bunch of buckets that are always good for something. They got the remaining Faber boat burning good.

"If people knew how much fun this was, everybody would be doing it all the time," Elizabeth sang. And that open-front boathouse went almost in a single blast of flame when they got it started. It burned sizzling down to the very water.

The Dulantys hoisted sail and fared out upon the blue bosom of Crow Creek. And they had timed it perfectly. It clouded over suddenly at sunset, and the dark fell down on everything like a curtain. They passed the returning Faber fishermen in that dark, all Dulanty noises being masked by the Fabers' loud and excited cursing at seeing the glow of flames around their own place.

The Dulantys passed so close that one hurried Faber oar actually banged the hull of the low-lying *Ile de France*. Then the Dulantys glided downstream, and in no time at all they were at the confluence of the waters, and immediately they were on the Green River itself.

It was night, and a memorable one. To be on the Green River was not really to be at sea, but to the Dulanty children it was very like a first night at sea.

They moored in the tightest and most covered cove of all. Trees came down low and pretty well screened them, and they were hidden well enough with the help of the darkness.

On that night there happened things of such variety and so out of every context that it almost seemed that they could not all be true. There were six major complexes of events; each happening when only one child was awake to observe and partake, and the rest were asleep. We are able to give only that which occurred to Helen; not that it was the most remarkable, on the contrary that it is the easiest to believe. The other five (Bad John did not remember anything unusual happening) had all said their sagas, and Helen moved easily into hers.

"There were ships came up Green River," she told,

"real ships. Peter hinted at something like this in his on silly story, but he did not get the big picture. I believe he was half awake for a short moment only while it was happening, and then he dreamed the rest of his. Well, these were really big ships, as I could tell by their outline between me and the trees and the stars. You may ask me how really big ships could come up Green river, and I believe I am able to answer you. They were remarkable shallow-draft vessels, a hundred feet high some of them, and drawing only two foot of water. They were pirate craft, and they were built that way for easier raiding up rivers and tidal estuaries.

"There was the *Spanish Dancer*. That was a ship! It is the fastest ship in the world. It can go twice the speed of the wind because of the way they reef its sails. It has the bloodiest pirates of all on it, except for the *Flying Snake* which has even bloodier ones. I went onto the *Spanish Dancer* and as soon as they realized my worth they made me captain. They said that, with my own courage added to their complement, they would even be able to whip the *Flying Snake* which was lurking down Green River for them.

"After I had established order on the *Spanish Dancer* and delegated authority, I got in a binnacle and rowed to investigate some of the other ships that were around here. I went on the *Vampire*, whose crewmen are served every night a cup of blood with their scuttle of rum. This is the ship that they had really taken Peter on, but he was sleepy and scared and he got the name wrong. They didn't actually take a gallon of his blood. They took only about a thimbleful to see what they had there. 'Oh Hell,' their blood-man said when he had run it through the tests, 'this kid's a Puca. We can't be drinking Puca blood; we got a contract with them says we don't drink their blood and they don't drink ours. I thought he was an Earth kid.' They put Peter to sleep then and carried him back to the *Ile* and put him in his bunk. And that's all in the world that happened to Peter. All the rest he told is lies.

"Hey, I stayed with those guys a long time and drank a lot of blood. Any of you ever drink a Bloody Mary or a Redhead made with real blood? I bet tomato juice will never do a thing for me again. They begged me to be their captain; and I had to slip away quietly, as I hate sticky goodbyes.

"Then I went onto the *Gigantis Transfixus*, the same ship that Fulbert told us about once. It is the tallest ship of all, and there is this about it that you cannot say about any other ship in the world: its mainmast is a man! The mainmast is a giant that the pirates captured in the Persian Gulf; and they made him stand there with his arms outstretched. All the yardarms and sails and things are spiked onto him. The way they got him to stand there was to put a spell on him for thirty years. His time was already up, but he didn't know it. Once a year they showed him a calendar, but it was an old calendar with a lot of time to go on it. The rest of the time they kept him blindfolded so he couldn't count the days.

"The giant is old now, and he's simpleminded, or he wouldn't have let them put the spell on him in the first place. The pirates were mean to him and they hadn't given him a drink of water for five years. We heard him moaning when we moored last night, but we didn't know what it was. He was the moaning we heard up in the treetops.

"I set it all to rights. I dipped a davit full of water and climbed up and gave him a drink. 'Thank you, Helen,' he said, 'that sure is good.' 'You count three,' I said, 'and then bust all those spikes and things out. You can be free now, thanks to Helen, because your time is up. And I wi?

back up your claim with mind and sinew.' Then I whistled for the men from the *Spanish Dancer* to come, as the men on the *Transfixus* were shooting at me and hitting me too. Then the giant busted out all the spikes that were sticking in him, and the whole superstructure of the *Transfixus* went down just as the men from the *Spanish Dancer* swarmed on board, and at the same time there was an explosion below decks and flames billowed everywhere—''

''Pirates are perhaps the greatest invention of Earth people,'' Elizabeth interrupted loftily, ''and their pirate stories are wonderful entertainment for small children. We have to give Earth people credit for that, they invented pirates.''

''—staunched the blood by a trick I'd learned from a Hindu lama years before,'' Helen was continuing, ''and picked up my left eye from the deck to replace it later. Then, taking an old toggle harpoon—''

''Uncle Henry says that Earth People invented pirates, but they used Pucas for a model,'' Peter said. ''He says that Bartholomew Portuguese was a Puca, and so was Teach (Blackbeard). They were doing a little irregular trade on Earth, and people modeled the pirate stories on them. But the second-rate pirates like Kidd were Earthmen.''

It was almost dawn and almost time for breakfast. Helen was still telling how she had sewed her severed arms back on, first the right and then the left, with a sail needle and gut-string made of the bowels of one of the slaughtered *Transfixus* seamen.

''How could you have sewed the right arm on first if you didn't have your left arm on to sew with?'' Dorothy asked.

''I just said that to see if you were paying attention,''

Helen said. "I really sewed my left arm on first and then my right."

You only think there ain't hidden inlets on Green River till it means your life to find one. The Dulantys found one (much better than their night mooring) when they heard the Fabers coming looking for them just before dawn. They got the *Ile* and the *Sea Bear* both into an inlet and secured them. And even the Fabers who knew every splash of those waters missed them. Charles was afraid that Catherine de Medici would make an outcry, but that goat was smart; she knew she'd go into the pot if the Fabers caught her. But the Fabers came so near that you could see their hard black eyes. It was a long time before those Fabers gave up the search.

The Dulantys lay in their branch-covered inlet all day. Sheriff Train came looking for them in a boat, calling out to them in a friendly fashion. Mr. Crocker came looking for them in a crazier boat with the three bloodhounds and the other dogs in it, and he let them out to snuffle the shore every few feet. And another bunch of Fabers came looking for them, and then another bunch.

And yet the children were able to catch and eat great strings of fish as they lay hidden. So the taunt of the Stinkers had been right! They did eat raw fish! Don't knock it till you've tried it.

And after they found out what made Catherine de Medici so cranky, they milked her and had goat milk to go with the choc beer for an original drink. This was the life, laced with adventure, sweetened with danger, full of challenge. They were as secure in their inlet as a turtle in its carapace, and the whole world could look for them forever and not find them.

That's why they were so surprised when, just after dark

of that second night, Phoebe Jane Lanyard was on the *It* before they saw or heard her.

"Now you kids listen to me and stop making trouble," she said before they could get in a word. "I saw Frank just an hour ago and told him that you were all right and that I would watch out for you. I went and talked to Hank in jail today, and I went up and saw Witchy for a little while. Things look bad for all three of them.

"You will have to stay hid. And you will have to stop burning down people's houses. It makes them mad. I brought you a honeycomb and some Indian bread. I brought you a peck of corn, and some pancake flour. I brought you a frog fork, and a gunny sack to put the frogs in. And I brought you some pepper, and six eggs. Oh, I forgot to bring one for you, Bad John! I'll bring you two tomorrow night. Which one of you is cook?"

"Myself, until I can train one of the younger children," said Helen.

"But you're the youngest of them all, Helen," Pheobe said. "Oh, I forgot, forgive me. You don't mean chronological age, do you? I forget just what it is you do mean. I brought you some shot for the .22 you stole from the Stinkers and the .30 you stole from Fiddler. I brought you a blacksnake to play with, and a bar of soap."

"How could you find us when even the Fabers couldn't?" Peter asked.

"Oh, they're only Cherokees. I wonder God doesn't take their eyes away from them since they never use them. What if smart Indians came looking for you? I'll have to hide you in a better place where everybody in the world can't see you when they go by."

"But Sheriff Train and Mr. Crocker looked for us, and the dogs too, and they couldn't find us," John said.

"Why, they're not even Indian (except that dog Candle

is one-quarter Seneca Indian); how could they find any-body? They have to use both hands to find the noses on their faces. Cast off now! We have to move!''

Pheobe Jane piloted them down the river about a mile. She put them in an inlet so hidden that the stars didn't even shine. It was like the inside of a blind shed.

''A family lived in this inlet for three generations once, and they never did see the sun,'' she said. ''The parents never saw the faces of their own children. It's do dark in here that you strike a match here and it shines dark instead of light. It's so dark here that you didn't see me go, and I left my voice here to talk with you for two minutes after I'm gone.''

And Pheobe Jane had indeed leapt lightly towards a probable shore and disappeared like a whisper into the total darkness.

''*A-wa-wa-shingay*,'' the Dulantys whispered after her.

The "Strife Dulanty" with the World

Little Jack Wilson—a poor man of Lost Haven—came and talked to Frank Dulanty one afternoon in the hills away from town. Little Jack didn't know how he had happened to meet Frank there, or even how he happened to be walking in the hills. But Frank knew. He had summoned Little Jack by means of a Bagarthach verse broadcast on the wind. You slant your verse to the man you are calling, and it will bring him almost every time.

"Little Jack, my family is lost and marooned and taken on all sides in a strange place," Frank said. "What do you think we should do?"

"I think you people should leave this region entirely, Frank," Little Jack told him, "though you seem to be the only one left to leave. You have no friends here. I'd like to be, but I'm scared on both sides: scared of you because I don't understand what kind of thing you are, and scared of the men of Lost Haven who will chop down anything that attaches to you. We sense you here as they wouldn't sense you in a larger or busier place. You look almost like eyeryone else, and damned if you don't act almost like everyone else—and I like you and your kindred better than I like anyone else in town. You've treated me decently and made me feel like a person, but I'm the butt of the lowest

Lost Haven clown of them all.

"But, Frank, you are different! And you devil us out of our minds with the difference. I don't know whether your brother killed Stutgard—I think not—but they'll kill him for that killing, and we both understand that. I don't know which of us are the sheep and which the goats, but we're of a different species. Get out of here, Frank!"

"What did you have in your mind to tell me, Little Jack, when you slid off up into the hills here? You had something on your mind to tell me?"

"Sure I had, Frank, and I have the feeling that you put it on my mind to come tell you what is going on."

"What is set in the minds of all of you? The time is tonight, I can read you that much, but what is the thing?"

"Ah—if I were you, Frank, I wouldn't be in that shanty of yours tonight at, say, ten o'clock," Little Jack said. "I would not light a light in that shanty at all tonight, and I would be out of it quickly after dark, if I went back to it at all. I'd stay in the hills if I were you. I'd watch it from some high vantage point and see what I might see."

"What would I see—them take myself out and hang me, Little Jack?"

"That's what you'd see if you can be in two places at one time, and I'm not sure that you can't. Aye, they intend to hang you—and it doesn't seem to bother you much. I'm told that you, whatever you are, do not fear death."

"Oh, we don't mind going when it's time to go, Little Jack. But we don't like being told by our lessers that it's time to go. And this hanging, for personal reasons I wish to avoid it. I tell you, any man or group that wants to hunt us like prey, we will make it an interesting hunt. And that goes for Crocker's Crocks. We've plenty of sporting blood in us. We'll make it fun."

"And sober up, Frank," Little Jack said. "It's your

life they'll require of you.''

"I *have* sobered up, Little Jack. Not a drop for two days now, though your world has always seemed a little bleak without it. What afflicts me is something else.''

The men of Lost Haven believed that Frank Dulanty was still on the drunk, as he had been immediately after the death of his wife, and that he could be handled easily. He wavered in his walk like a drunk, and he had the flushed look and the hot eye of a drunk. But he was sober as a Rogers County judge. It was the Earth Allergy that had caught up with him and sent him along reeling and sick, that would kill him soon if something else didn't do it first.

But real sporting blood can bubble up even through Earth Allergy. Frank would give them a run for it. There would be fun for all.

It was not completely dark till after nine that night. And the men came long before ten. It was very close.

It was so close that Frank, sliding out of his darkened shanty by a loosened plank that only he and little Helen knew about, mingled with the men in front of the shanty and mingled his voice in with theirs in Lost Haven accents. (All Pucas love to mimic.) It was very dark there. It had better be.

The men had several ropes, and they made a lot of noise asking each other who had them and if they were all set.

Crocker arrived then, giving orders. He was the man who gave all the orders in Lost Haven, now that Stutgard was dead.

"Go in and get him," Crocker snapped. A dozen men were heaving up a heavy twelve-by-twelve to use for a battering ram on the door. Crocker let them get their momentum up, then twisted the knob, flicked open the unlocked door, and let the twelve men and their balk crash on their faces into the shanty. Some of them are still picking splinters out of their jowls today.

Crocker was smart, and he enjoyed doing things like that to his men. But he knew that Frank Dulanty would devise something more intricate than a barred door. He suspected a trap of some sort inside, and sending twelve men crashing in like that with a heavy timber would be enough to spring most traps.

Crocker went in after the men. They lit the lights in the shanty, and they seemed to search the place pretty thoroughly. The expectation fell in the men outside. Too long a time in there. The man had skipped, that was plain.

"No show tonight," Joe Cottonhead grumbled outside. Cottonhead was another poor man of Lost Haven.

"No, I just don't believe they'll find me in there, Joe," Frank Dulanty said low to Cottonhead who was standing beside him in the dark.

"Is it yourself, Frank?" Cottonhead asked even lower. "You have nerve. I could call them out and have them over here, but I've always been afraid of you and your brother; I don't know what you'd do to me before the other men got here. What do you want now?"

"The same thing you want, Joe, a show. You said there wouldn't be one tonight. There will. I've just picked the spot for it, partly with yourself in mind.

"A man with a thirst like yours isn't all bad, Joe. It shows you're still alive. I know where you want to be, and we'll have it there. I'll slip off now and check the script. And here's what you do: When the men are tired of playing around here and not finding me, you just sing out 'Everybody over to Blind Ben's Bar! Drinks are for everybody!' Tell them that somebody will be along to pick up the tab in a little while, and I will be. If Crocker talks about getting the dogs to track me down, you sing out 'Everybody over to Blind Ben's Bar! Start the manhunt from there!'"

Frank Dulanty slipped away then, and Joe Cottonhead began to bawl: "Everybody over to Blind Ben's. We got a live one in a minute."

Crocker and his men finally decided that Frank was hid nowhere in the shanty. They came out and left the lights on and the doors open. Blind Ben's Bar sounded all right to Crocker also, if there was a live one somewhere to pick up the tab.

"I'll get the dogs after we've all had a drink," he said. And the bunch of them, about twenty men in all, started to Blind Ben's.

"Is it you, Frank? You can't jump us all?" It was Little Jack Wilson who had lagged behind.

"I can if I time it right," Frank said. "Go along after them, Little Jack. I'll make my entrance shortly. The show will be worth it."

Frank entered his own shanty boldly. He went to the only place Crocker had gone, though Crocker's men had gone everywhere. On his own bed (Crocker was himself a little fey to know for sure which was Frank's bed in the shanty) Frank found a rope with a noose. It was heavy and neat and well tied, and attached was an obscene and taunting note. Crocker had a gift for this too. If he's been a Puca, he'd have put it into verse, but it was essentially a Bagarthach.

Frank sat down for a few moments and tapped with his foot as though counting time. He felt better by the second; the Earth Sickness flowed away from him and he became a real Puca again. He began to grin, a mean crooked grin that he seldom used, a grin that would back off even his brother Henry.

In Lost Haven they hadn't thought of Frank as a giant, since they had usually seen him with his heavier and uglier brother—the one who really spooked them. But Frank was a long, strong man, larger than life, and unbelievably swift. He had the sudden tide in him—as have all Pucas and many Earthmen—and it rose up now; the essence of that tide is power and timing. And he had, when he wished to use it, what the Puca call the *Fianaise*—the Presence. Frank was capable of his moments.

Frank took the note, and the rope with its noose. He went out of the shanty, still leaving all doors open and all lights on. He went toward Blind Ben's Bar.

A man had gone for Crocker's dogs, and he was bringing them across that rough little milo field on the south end of town. They were booming and baying as they worked up to their own sort of excitement. Frank knew exactly when they got the cross-wind whiff of him. He heard them cower and refuse.

Then he knew that he was at full effect. The dogs were afraid of him, and their men would be. He came the last steps with a lion-swiftness, entering Blind Ben's with much more noise than was necessary, banging the door back with a heavy clatter. He stood there with the noosed rope in his hands. He had studied it out in his mind just where the hanging lantern in Blind Ben's would light him most effectively, and he made that a part of his timing when he jumped them. The men drew in breath like bayed badgers, and they stiffened like dogs.

"Holy horse-hocks!" breathed Sad Sam Burns. "It's The Dulanty!"

Frank held them all rigid for a long moment, drained them dry, and then released them—except the whitefaced

Crocker.

"Take your ease," Frank said. "Everybody drinks but Crocker. Set them up, Ben. It's a celebration."

"Who'll pay?" Blind Ben asked doggedly. "They've been bugging me that there's a live one coming."

"I'll pay, Ben," Frank said, "and then I'll pay off someone else."

Ben set the drinks out, beer and choc beer, horse whisky and crooked-neck jug whisky, turnip brandy and granny wine. The men glowed into them as to a feast and fell to it.

"Crocker, back up half a step!" Frank ordered suddenly in a throaty whisper that was so loud that it echoed. That throaty thing was always threatening and effective when used with Earthmen. And Crocker fell back half a step.

Frank Dulanty whistled a little tune in an unearthly key. He went over to the scared Crocker, put the noose around his neck and fitted it snug. He tossed the end of the line over a rafter and pulled it tight.

"Some of you men take this fool!" Crocker babbled. "Sad Sam, you've got your rifle. Take it and level on this—" But Frank pulled the line tighter and cut off Crocker's words.

The men all watched it like a show. This Crocker, be it understood, was no patsy. He was a rough man who handled killer dogs. He had been running the town for Stutgard and running it by force. Now he had intended to run it for himself.

Frank unraveled a paper from his pocket and presented it in front of Crocker's now ashen face, at the same time slackening the line a little. Crocker tore the noose with his hands till he could breathe again. Nobody had realized what a tall craggy man Frank was, nor that he had such great hands on him.

71

"Did you write this note?" Frank asked Crocker.

"No, I swear to God I didn't, Frank," Crocker blurted. "Some of you men take this animal! There's enough of you. Surely twenty men can handle one of him!"

' But the men would not be done out of their show. They were liking this. "He wrote it. Crocker wrote it," several of them volunteered.

"If you wrote it, eat it," Frank ordered, and he stuffed it into Crocker's mouth. Crocker's eyes boggled and he closed his mouth on the paper, but he still looked stubborn.

"I said *Eat it!*" Frank cried angrily. He gave a strong pull on the line and half strangled Crocker. Crocker's jaws began to move to save his neck. He swallowed. His Adam's-apple popped like a cork and the note was down.

Frank jerked the billfold from Crocker's pocket and threw it on the bar. "Keep the drinks coming till it's used up," he told Blind Ben. "Crocker promised these men a show tonight, and this is the least he can do for them.

"—But you can have none!" he said fiercely to Crocker who was still noosed. "Your tongue must stay dry for a while. And just let me see the color of it, I've heard that it's black."

Frank pulled on the rope till Crocker showed the color of his tongue. It was not black; it was muted red.

"Go home now, Crocker," Frank said, drawing the line back across the rafter. "But leave the noose around your neck and the rope trailing you in the street. I will have eyes following you to report it if you do not. Don't take it off till you're in your own house. And keep it handy. Whenever I am ready I will send for you, and you will bring it, and I will complete the job. But that is not for tonight."

Crocker left, still white with anger and fear, and he

72

trailed the rope behind him. That jackal-cat Crocker had been belled now, and he would be banged and hounded by things both within and outside himself.

Frank had timed the tide of Crocker and the men, and he took them all that easily. Now he slid easily into the drinking with the men, drawing on a fund of Puca-flavored stories and jokes to entertain them. They were his for tonight, but he couldn't have pulled such a trick again. He felt the Earth Sickness stealing back over him, and now he was less than a full Puca.

It had been a temporary thing, and he knew it. Oh, they'd still kill him, or one of their kind would. But he was the bear for a while, and they were the dogs. Was it possible that, for the short interval, he had seemed much larger than he was? Can the Puca fake such appearance?

Frank Dulanty was but little above average man-size, but all the men would remember him as some sort of giant in that episode.

The men of the town liked him more after this show, and yet it had become still more inevitable that they would kill him and his brother Henry. The Dulantys were almost-men. That's what spooks are.

Phoebe Jane Lanyard had gone to see Witchy at the institution at Vinita. Witchy was *not* all right. Her eyes did not focus properly, and the two sides of her face were different. But she was lively that day; and she recognized Phoebe, having always been a friend of the poor Indian woman. Witchy's voice was now like that of a small girl, perhaps her own daughter Helen:

"Phoebe, I've found a passage in Scripture that explains everything," she said. "It's by Saint John, so our faith constrains us to accept it:

> *"The Devil and Crocker and Stut*
> *Put all of their heads in one hat,*
> *And mixed them and added them up,*
> *And hadn't the brains of a cat."*

"I don't think Saint John really wrote that, Witchy," Phoebe said. "You just made it up."

"Oh? I thought it was in the Apocalypse, but maybe not. The Apocalypse and me are a lot alike. There's another one, I think it's from Tertullian:

> *"The Devil sent Crocker for Stut*
> *To bring him his head on a plate.*
> *The Devil said 'I'm in a rut,*
> *That's something I oughtn't to ate.'"*

"I don't believe anyone wrote that either, Witchy. You just made it up."

"Well, maybe so. I make up verses all day long. Sometimes real dirty ones. I wonder why. I wish Veronica would bring the coffee."

"Veronica is dead, Witchy."

"Don't *you* start giving me that funny look, Phoebe. I know she's dead. I still wish she'd bring the coffee. They won't let me have any more, just because I always bend up the spoons and break the cups when I'm through with them. Can you get me out of here, Phoebe?"

"Sure, I can shuck you over the wall easily enough after dark. We'll pick a night real soon, Witchy."

"Phoebe," Witchy said in a suddenly rational moment, "there's several other people of our sort in the United States. I wonder if you could get in touch with them. I hate for the family to be broken up and the kids spilled into the world as young as they are. That might not be safe."

"What are the addresses of these others, Witchy?"

"Oh, we don't keep addresses. The only contact we have with each other is of an informal and intuitive sort."

"Well, haven't they at least names?"

"Oh, Wily McGilly, Diogenes Pontifex, John Pandemonium, Aloysius Shiplap, names like that. They're important people, scientists and musicians and confidence men and such. Hell, you're a Shawnee. You say that Shawnees can sense things as well as we can. Find one of them as a favor to me, Phoebe."

"All right. It had sprung up in my mind this morning like a mushroom that I would meet one of those names very soon. He's about a day's travel away and coming in this direction."

After that, Witchy had one of her attacks and was not coherent. Then she was much worse. She looked like something entirely different. She foamed and raved. No one had ever found fault with the people who had tied her up like a dog and brought her to the hospital that other night. She had been in such a state then.

Attendants brought Witchy under control, and told Phoebe that she would have to leave.

But this attack passed quickly. Witchy called out once more in her old-new little girl voice—

"Wait, Phoebe, there's one more—

> *"The Devil rolled Stut like a ball*
> *And said as he dropped in a hole,*
> *'It tickles my tail to recall*
> *The prices he charged us for coal.'* "

After that, Witchy was led back into the building, and they saw no more of each other that day.

"She didn't even ask about the children," Phoebe said to herself. "Maybe she thinks that Veronica is still taking care of them."

8

Was Mostly That They Didn't Fit It

There is one spot on the Green River that is always foggy. Even at midday there is so strong a haze that you can look straight at the sun, and it is blue. The fog comes from Misu Mound that stands on the right bank of Green River, though Helen said it was the left bank.

"When you face downriver, the left bank is the left bank," she told them. "Is that clear to everybody? But when you turn around and face upriver, then the left bank is the right bank and the right bank is the left bank."

"You can't make the right turn into the left bank just by turning around," Peter protested.

"Oh, but you can. The bank that you called the left bank when you faced downriver will be the left bank forever. I think there is an intenational covenant on that. But when you face upriver, the left bank will be on your right hand, so the ignorant will call it the right bank."

"The only place it is still the left bank when it is on your right is in the left lobe of your brain." Peter argued stubbornly. "I suspect the Helen-brain is mostly left lobe."

Well, the Dulanty children had to look upriver to Misu Mound from their hidden inlet, and from there Misu Mound was on the right-hand bank even if Helen called it the left bank.

The mound had been started by people older than the Shawnees, so Phoebe Jane didn't really know much more about it than the Dulantys did. She faked a lot of her stuff. But she told them that this was the way the mound was made:

First they lay a number of dead people out on the ground. A lot of them weren't ready to go, Phoebe Jane had told them, but you can't start a mound with only two or three dead bodies. Then you put whatever you think the dead people would enjoy with them, and bring dirt and cover them up. The next year you bury more people on top of them, and in a very few centuries you have a mound. But the fact is that there was something there below the ground when they started. You don't build a mound just anywhere.

If you dig deep there, even today, below the level of the surrounding ground and under the mound itself, you will find the bones of unknown animals.

Phoebe Jane's uncle once dug out a set of those bones and took them over to the University. He thought he was performing a service, as University people are supposed to be interested in things like that. But those hangdog professors looked at him like he was the weird one. They went over those bones snuffling like a bunch of dogs, and they seemed to get madder the more they snuffled.

"You didn't find these bones all together," one of the professors gruffed at him. "There couldn't be an animal like this. The shoulder bone is from a deformed buffalo, or perhaps an exceptionally heavy angus. The ribcage is from an old plowhorse whose skeleton you must have found in a pasture somewhere. Both are about fifty years old. These are bear's jaws. The hindquarters are from a jack, wouldn't you say so, Professor Elmo?''

"A jack or a mule certainly. He got them up in the big lime country, the only place that recent bones would be so well preserved on the surface, and the only place where joker Indians still obtain. These fangs are good ivory—too good. They're of common texture throughout—without a core. There never was a tooth without a core. What did you whittle them out of, man, a cue ball?''

"The fangs wouldn't go with the jaws,'' the other professor said, "and the jaws wouldn't go with this cow's skull that you have here; nor would a cow's skull attach with such neck bones as these: they're alligator's and have Barataria Bay Louisiana Recent written all over them. What were you ever doing in Louisiana, Indian, and how did you come by these?''

"I used to drive that territory for the Red Dog Truck Line,'' Phoebe's uncle had said, and it was the truth, he had.

"An altogether impossible animal,'' said one of the professors. "There ought to be a law against hoaxers. You didn't find all these bones together.''

"I by damn *did* find those bones all together,'' Phoebe's uncle said, "and there's hundreds of sets of them in the roots of Misu Mound.'' But the men didn't believe him.

It's true that Phoebe's uncle was an eight-ply liar who was also an elaborate practical joker. That's all right. Some of the greatest discoveries have been made by eight-ply liars. How did the men know there weren't other bones like that in Misu Mound if they didn't go and dig?

The layers of the mound differed from each other in what was buried there. In the first layer of the mound, every dead body had been buried with a horse. In the second layer, every body had been buried with a lion. These weren't tawny like the mountain lions of today; they were black and brindled. In the next layer, each body was buried with a buffalo. And very near the top, each body was buried with a Puca.

Then there came a day when the mound wouldn't hold another body. People had no more than scratched the sod to set in one more body when all the old dead people became very excited over the intrusion.

"Oh, go away and leave us alone," the old dead people grumbled, "we're full up here." And the dead buffalo grunted and the bears growled and the lions screamed and the Pucas sang Bagarthachs and the unknown animals at the botton rumbled like buried thunder and there was hell to pay all around. So they hadn't buried anybody in Misu Mound since then, except accidentally.

Much of this about the Mound was what Phoebe had told the children, but some of it they had told themselves. It was all true except one part: they sure never buried Pucas with people there like you would bury horses with them. Phoebe just put that in to rile them up because the Dulantys were Puca people.

Phoebe was the only Earth person who knew that the name of them was Puca—a word the children were never to use to outsiders. And they hadn't told it to her. Phoebe knew some things of herself.

But how was it that Veronica and Witchy had used to tell the children similar stories about mounds back home? Misu Mound resembled the mounds in the Puca country in ways that Phoebe didn't know about.

There was a big room in the middle of Misu Mound. Nobody but the Dulanty children knew about that room, fifty feet down below the top of the mound; and they were able to go directly to it by passages unknown to others. The Puca in their native surroundings lived as much under the ground as on top of it. The Puca, as a matter of fact, did not, strictly speaking, resemble goblins; it was kobolds they looked like, but these are not so well known to Earth people.

It was in this big room that the dead people would gather and sit and talk when they were tired of lying in one position. They cracked old bones to get the marrow, and they drank corn beer. It didn't take much eating and drinking to keep them up, since they were no longer fleshed. They didn't eat much, but they sure did smoke a lot. It is not generally known, but dead people used tobacco for centuries before live people stumbled onto it. That had also been the case with the Puca. The smoke all came out through a hole in the side of the mound, and that caused the fog or haze.

The children learned the interior of the mound. They could have hidden there from all pursuit, but they couldn't have taken their rafts there. They dug all over the flanks of the mound, and came out with bones of animals and people. They dug out two prime skulls which they set up on the prows of their rafts.

The children formed enduring friendships with many of the old Indians in the middle of Misu Mound. They learned a lot about Earth people from them, how they are in their essence, what are the real things that are hidden under the daily exterior, and how it was in the old days. And they learned the right way to cure tobacco and to make pipes and how really to smoke up a storm.

It came to Peter always just two hours before dawn. It came up out of the ground or out of the water like a land-wave or a sea-wave and possessed him completely. It was then that the Earth ambient brought it on him, too early, too green, too rank.

And it was then that the sea-hammock itself became evil; and he had to come out of it, trembling and sick—to do anything, anything: to roll on the deck in the dark, or thrash onto the shore and go crashing through the thickets, cutting and barking himself till he could lick the blood off his own arms and taste it mixed with salt and the smell of bruised weeds—to think of it instead of the passion.

The early-morning passion of a goblin child raised on a hothouse planet is something that no Earthling will ever know. He belonged on a world where the months and years were different, and where balanced precocity was the rule. But here on the gray Earth there was something that at the same time inhibited and retarded the substance of it, while it forced the accidentals in untimely fashion. Peter was out of balance. He was sick with the wild surging sickness.

The children had not avoided the Earth Sickness entirely, certainly Peter had not. And the essence of Earth Sickness is the violent emotional revolt of interior passion against itself, its throttling by the inhibiting Earth ambient, and the subsequent regression into a listless lethargy as sometimes to be fatal in the case of adults. This turmoil is unexplained, but the Puca Anima in an Earth Matrix suffered from violent and misdirected yearnings of all sorts, and these were entangled with depressing frustrations.

But Peter would fight the violence with violence, going very deep into the water (it is cooler then, a little before dawn, than at any hour) down to the bottom and grab mud; staying for minutes and still more minutes until even Puca lungs were near to bursting and Peter would see red and purple under water.

Then he'd turmoil up and break surface and violently swim his fill, stroking for an hour or more back and forth across the river, trying to tire himself and finding it impossible.

Afterwards, when white morning came, he would swim back to the *Ile*, go aboard, dress, and start breakfast, cured and at peace now until the next foredawn. In the daytime a goblin can pass for human or any other harmless species.

But Peter knew that he could no longer wrestle with his beautiful cousins Elizabeth and Helen, or dive off their shoulders, or even go swimming or unclothed with them until, perhaps, this thing should leave him.

In the daylight he would look closely at the others and wonder if they had ever known the passion. Elizabeth had not; he would have known it if she had. He watched Charles, and he knew that he had not. Dorothy hadn't, or John. Bad John, if he had known it at all, could not by his nature have known it in the same way.

Then Peter looked at Helen and he wasn't sure. It was quite possible with her. She was younger than the rest, but she was weird. And in all other ways she was precocious.

Then she looked at him the same way he was looking at her, and they were both scared.

83

A priest came to see Henry Dulanty in his cell. He was an old Holland Dutchman, not one of your new young priests who doesn't know an Analect from the Anastasis.

He found Henry reading and was surprised at the book he had.

"It's almost like a staged thing that I should find you with that," the old priest said, "nearly a touch of the phony there. Where are you reading?"

"Maerens incedebam sine furore, consurgens in turba clamabam."

"Og, from Job. It goes on 'I was the brother of dragons and companion of ostriches. My skin is become black upon me. My harp is turned to mourning.' I had a professor once who called him the Majestic Cry-Baby. You aren't, are you?"

"Yes, a little. We luxuriate in our misfortunes more than do the people of—that is—more than—"

"More than do the people of Earth, Dulanty? I guessed you as soon as I came in. In a long life, I believed I had encountered it twice before, but I wasn't sure. With you I am. You're from an alien world. But it's odd that an alien should be reading Latin."

"Father, our briefing was a few centuries out of date, I believe. Latin, and three American Indian tongues (which I cannot identify with any presently known), were the only Earth languages I learned before I came to Earth. As to this work, I have become quite interested in Earth mythology. It is intimated in this that the Anointed *(Fear-ungadh-mac,* as we would say in our own language) would be born in Coelo-Syria in a town hardly to be called a city. In the latter part of this anthology, it is made out that he has already been born. Our own teaching is that the

84

Anointed will be born on the meanest of worlds, hardly to be called a world. Some have surmised that it may be Earth, but this interpretation isn't widely held. Nor do we believe that he has been born yet, but you never know about these things. Comparative mythology is interesting."

"Sometimes I believe that you people (I've had a notion about you people for a long time) appear in Scripture," the old priest said. "As 'In those days there were giants on Earth.' "

"Oh, that's us all right," Henry said. "Some of us have been here before, small bunches quite a few times through the millennia. But in the latter part of this there are passages where Paul seems to be writing from our viewpoint. 'Do you not know that we shall judge Angels?' he writes. How do you interpret that, Father? To you it can't make sense. Do you judge Angels?"

"Do you?"

"Yes, sometimes, when they fall within our jurisdiction. Our contact with them, however, is nothing like what you might imagine; they themselves are nothing like what you might imagine. I'm surprised that Earth people have even heard of them, but several are in this tome under their own proper names. There are a number of other things in this collection that make sense when applied to us, but not when applied to you. It beats me how you can understand this book at all."

"It beats me too, Dulanty," the priest said. "I'd like to talk about it longer, but I suspect that neither of us is going to live very much longer. I'm supposed to be here to bring you solace, but I'd rather try to study you out a little. As far back as our seminary days we were posed the interesting question: What if we should somewhere encounter intelligent aliens? Was salvation for them also? Or only for those of the human recension? Now I've come onto you and I don't know where to begin. I look at you and I ask whether I can ever enter into an alien mind and think as it thinks. Can any man ever understand any alien?''

"I ask the same question," Henry said. "From my viewpoint, I'm the man, you're the alien. How weird are the ways of Earth! Or as it is written, 'Can anything good come from Earth?' ''

"The jailer is banging on the bars down there, Dulanty. He hates you and is afraid of you. He won't give you much time with anyone. Ah, Dulanty, do Puca confess? They're going to kill you, you know, either inside or outside the lines.''

"Yes, we confess. Try and stop one of us sometime. As we come to our end, we are not the Majestic Cry-Babies, but we are the most Bumptious Babblers you ever encountered. We confess; if a *Sagart* is not available, then to an ordinary Puca; if a Puca is not available, then to an inhabitant of Astrobe, or to a Camiroi, or even to an Earthman; if no cogent person is available, then to a dromedary or a dog or a mole or a tree or a stone.''

"Begin then, my distant cousin.''

"I'll warn you, though, Father. You are an old man. It might kill you. There are deeper and darker places in us than in you. We do sometimes treat so loosely with—''

"Tell me, and do not be afraid. I have heard everything.''

Henry Dulanty confessed to the old priest, and it did kill him. Not immediately, but it killed him. That old man only thought that he had heard everything. Even though the priest suspected, in one corner of his mind that remained clear, that he had fallen afoul of a master storyteller who was having him on, yet the creature was having him on to his death and perhaps to his damnation. As the Dulanty reeled off his spiel, the mind of the old man seemed to melt like wax. It was lost in a strangeness more frightful than any evil he had ever suspected. The talking creature was an almost-man, but he flicked his ears like an animal and showed green billowing flames behind his eyes.

Henry Dulanty wasn't mean—for a Puca. But he felt the compulsion to confess and the black delight that it brought him. He'd warned the old fellow that it might kill him.

The old priest retched weakly and groaned and hung onto the bars. The jailer led him out of the cell and out of the building, and left him shaking and stuttering in the street.

The priest was in too much of a turmoil to drive his car. He hired a young fellow to drive him home. He then phoned the bishop that he was no longer able to perform his duties, and that he should be allowed to go to the Old Priests' Home.

He died there a month later.

9

No Setting for the Gallant Brood

The children did not think of their parents as being any longer of the immediate living. They considered them as having gone through that passage that is a tighter and darker crawl than any of the tunnels in Misu Mound, and as having come into the Central Room itself; or, if not having actually arrived there, as being well on the way.

"After your parents die they turn into your ancestors," Helen said. "They call it metamorphosis."

Now the Dulanty children thought of their parents as having already become their ancestors.

Veronica was already dead. Witchy was in the boobyhatch, and she always said that she would die if she were shut up. Maybe she'd die tonight. Maybe she was already dead.

Henry was in jail, and everybody knew that he would be killed. He joked about it himself, Phoebe had told them. Frank was dying of the Earth Sickness, but not dying fast enough; the men would still come some dark night and kill him too before the other thing killed him.

It was like an old Puca comedy, one person falls into the quicksand, and then drags a second one in after him, and then a third and a fourth, till they all disappear to their deaths. Who could help laughing at a thing like that, especially when the actors were of another people than the Puca and had been given parts in the play which were real? The children, having lived all their lives on Earth, had not actually seen any of the traditional Puca comedies, but they knew all about them.

So, they could consider the elder Dulantys as gone. Had it not been for this, there would have been a problem. The children were still committed to reducing the world to a population of six, or seven if you count Bad John. They couldn't stay in the nest forever. They were entitled to a world of their own. And time was solving, had solved in their minds, the problem for them.

Peter slipped off one day while the search for them was intense. He went back into Lost Haven while the Lost Haven kids were out looking for them in the hills and bogs and pits. He snugged up his ears tight, and he made himself as blank-faced as any Earth kid you'd ever seen. He even shambled along like one of them instead of walking brightly. He went to the Dulanty shop truck with all its tools and jigs and lathes, and he made a gadget. He brought it back and gave it to Charles who had thought that it might come in handy. Peter was a better fabricator than any of the rest of them.

If Sheriff Tolliver Train couldn't find the children, and if Mr. Crocker couldn't find them with his bloodhounds, it still didn't mean that they couldn't be found. Crocker would rather the children should be lost forever, but he couldn't have them popping up unexpectedly; he had to know where they were before he could know where he was. Crocker now used another sort of bloodhounds. He hired blackbirders or impressors for a dollar a day to find them. And the impressors found them on the third or fourth day.

The blackbirders were children of Lost Haven. Children? They were as big as houses; some of them were eleven years old. They were led by two really big boys with shotguns. They beat the woods and prowled the streams, and quartered and back-tracked, and really searched systematically. They also employed hunch and imagination. These had been their own woods and streams before the Dulantys had intruded, and they'd show those wogs who was tops at this game.

The two big eleven-year-old boys were Baxter Bushyhead and Little Sad Sam Jones (the son of Sad Sam Jones himself). They had one middle-sized boy with them when they struck the true trail and came onto the Dulantys.

It happened that the Dulantys had been night-owling it around and in Misu Mound the night before, and now they were sleeping up in the daytime. Even their watch, Dorothy, had gone to sleep.

The impressors worked it perfect, and they had the drop on them: two leveled shotguns trained on them before they knew what had happened, and a little carbine thing held by the middle-sized boy, Harold Harvestman, who was as spindly as one.

The Dulantys were shamed to be taken like that, and they had to stall while the little wheels in their heads whirled and meshed.

"We got you cold," Baxter Bushyhead shouted. "Come on shore and start marching."

"We get a nine dollar bonus!" Little Sad Sam Jones whooped. "That's a woolly bunch of money. And Baxter and me each get twice as much of it as Harold because we're leaders. I'd like to know how much that'll get me."

"Three dollars and sixty cents," Peter said, watching for a break in their front. "But if you knock Harold off in

91

the water and hold him under while he drowns you'll each get four dollars and a half. I'll watch your guns for you while you do it.''

"Ah, we hadn't better, he's my cousin," Baxter said. "All right now, you kids, come on shore and start marching. We'll blast you to pieces if you don't get to moving right now.''

"It's a pity you're imperfect," Helen said, looking steadily at Baxter Bushyhead.

"What do you mean, imperfect?" Baxter wanted to know.

"I was thinking of your skull," Helen explained. "It's misshapen. It's a lot of work to prepare a skull, and yours won't be a prime one when we've finished with it. It'll have some interesting contours, but there's too many things against it. Was your head always funny-shaped like that?''

"Say, where *do* you get those skulls?" Baxter snapped at the bait. "You got any more of them?"

"Sure we have," Helen said. "We'll trade you three of ours for your three, and the ones we have here are already fixed up. We get the skulls off of people. Where else? Those two on the prows of our rafts are from the two men who thought they had the drop on us yesterday. I worked till late into the night fixing them up.''

"What you do with them? How you fix them?" Little Sad Sam Jones was interested too.

"Well, to start with, we first sever the head completely from the body with our cutlasses. If the neck is too tough, we've got a bone saw. Then we slice off the ears. Ears are a terrible nuisance when you're fixing up a skull, and the only things that will take them as bait are turtles.''

"What you do next?" Baxter demanded.

"Empty out the brains. Everybody says you don't have

92

any, Baxter, but I'm betting there'll be good solid meat we can use in your head. I'm on your side. We use the brains for bait, and big boys' brains are the best. You can really catch catfish with brains if you know your business. Show them the big catfish we caught with those last brains, John."

John went into the *Ile's* cabin for them. He was the dumbest of the boys, but Helen never suspected that he could slip on that one. But what he brought out of the cabin was a string of catfish, just as she'd told him. Helen almost popped.

It was a good string of cats with several really big ones. The string of fish weighed as much as John did. Baxter Bushyhead and his blackbirders were impressed by it; but John couldn't understand the look of pure hatred that Helen turned on him, or the sneering malevolence with which Charles and Peter and Elizabeth regarded him. He had done what Helen had asked him to. This was no time to play riddles with people having the drop on you.

"You caught all those with brains?" Baxter asked.

"We sure did," Helen told him. "We should get twice as many this afternoon, what with so much fresh bait that's walked right into our trap. Well, the next thing you do when you make a skull is pull the eyes out and set them aside. You remember what we always do with the eyes, Charles?"

"I sure do," Charles said, "and I know what I'd like to do with another pair of eyes." But he was looking at John rather than at Helen, and he had an icy look that scared John.

"What do you do then?" Baxter asked, and Helen had him hypnotized.

"Oh, then we make a bunch of incisions in just the right places. We peel the flesh off the skull just like taking off a pair of gloves. Then we hand the skull overboard in a net and let the fish clean off the scraps of meat. After that, we pull it in and wash it three times, once in salt water, once in vinegar, and once in fresh water. Then we rub it with lime and set it in the sun to whiten.''

''And they come out like that in just one day?''

''Oh, much less. We'll have yours finished in less than an hour, Baxter. We will keep yours for comic effect, even if it is misshapen. Unfortunately you won't be able to see it.''

''Why won't I be able to see it?'' Baxter asked.

''You won't have anything left to see it with. We'll have your eyes in the eye jug, and you won't be in your skull anymore.''

''Oh, I forgot.'' Baxter seemed a little bewildered. ''But what do you use the eyes for? You said it was something special.''

''Eyes are the best bait of all. We catch garfish with them. Charles, step into the cabin and get one of those three-foot-long garfish to show them.''

Charles darted in, and he brought it out quickly. It was a good three foot long; but if it was a garfish it was a .30 caliber one. Charles had the drop on the blackbirders suddenly, with the rifle at ready and ready to talk business. Say, those big kids dropped their guns fast when they were given the order in the proper way. Crocker's three hirelings had been hypnotized by the honied voice of Helen, and Charles caught them flat. The Dulantys had added two shotguns and a carbine to their arsenal, and they had three prisoners to dispose of.

Baxter Bushyhead and his bunch could reach pretty high when told to reach, and they could march pretty fast when told to march. Charles, telling Peter and John that he needed no help, marched the three prisoners back into the woods. They were gone a very long time, and then Charles returned alone.

"Did you kill them?" Elizabeth asked.

"All dead and disposed of," Charles said. "It's no great trick for a man. The next time I'll let one of the boys do it."

"We didn't hear any shots," Helen said suspiciously.

"I used a silencer."

"You don't have a silencer. Where is it now?"

"I keep it hid. It's against the law in this state to use a silencer when you kill somebody."

But Helen wasn't satisfied with the explanation. For one thing, Charles was fingering some dollar bills, and Helen knew that Crocker had been paying his blackbirders a dollar a day to find them.

"Where did you get that money, Charles?" she demanded. "It's blood money, and we want our share of it. If you took it off their dead bodies, part of it belongs to us. If you took it from them as a bribe not to kill them, that's dishonest; but we still want some of it."

"I took some of it off them, and some of it was a bunch of old money that I already had. Sure, part of it belongs to each of you. I've marked it for you. But I've just made myself treasurer of this outfit and I'll handle the money for you all. That's because I know how to handle money better than the rest of you."

"How'll you prove you can handle money better than I can?" Helen asked.

"Because I'm the only one that's got any money. I handle mine this way. Let's see how you handle yours."

"I'm getting mighty blamed suspicious about the whole thing," Helen shrilled. "I think you're a crook and didn't kill them at all. If you let them go, they'll be back with help to get us.''

"They won't be back," Charles said.

"You just let me see that money. I can always tell dishonest money.''

"Yeah, I know, it's green on one side. You just leave it alone.''

Helen suspected that Charles had not killed those big boys at all.

Well, had he? Nobody had followed to see except Bad John, and nobody had thought to ask Bad John. But Charles did have a silencer. Peter had made it for him in the shop truck, and it worked better than any commercial silencer on the market.

And Charles had something else which he showed to John and Peter and Bad John, but not to the girls. There were three pair of the things, and they were gory.

"You will see, Peter, that these are considerably different from the flesh-colored pods of the Cherokee Creeper which an unnamed child once brought back to fool little girls,'' Charles said loftily.

If those three big boys were still walking around, they were walking around without any ears. Ears are one thing you can't fake. These were real Earth-kid ears.

Charles had taken a major step. You can't remain a child forever. Peter swallowed his jealousy and wryly dubbed his cousin Charles Earl of the Ears.

"I know why Helen and Charles looked at me like that,'' John said later. "I was supposed to get a gun in the cabin and get the drop on them. They got mad because I brought out the catfish instead.''

"I don't know why you got mad at John,'' Dorothy told them. "You told him to get the catfish. If you wanted him to get a gun, why didn't you tell him so?''

"Even six or seven persons may be too many in the world," Helen said evilly. "Shall we consider reducing our figure by two?"

But those blackbirders never came hunting the Dulantys again, not those three, nor any of the others who had been hunting elsewhere.

10

In Sacred Groves of Yew or Lindens

The children woke one morning as to the sounding of a horn off Earth. This is the horn that you hear, not with the physical ear, but with the interior one. "It is going to rain," Veronica used to say when a day dawned like that. "I can hear the tune of Bagarthach verses back home."

There was that feeling now—that there *was going to be* music. And by music, the Dulantys did not mean any such weak thing as the Earth people mean by that word. And lesser creatures also got the feel of the strong day.

The crows had gone crazy, staggering and hooting in the air as though ready to pack their bags and leave that country forever. Peter, who had been prowling around underwater before dawn, reported that the catfish were sealing their ears and digging into the bottom mud as though they had gone crazy.

Henry Dulanty had once given the opinion that the birds and animals of Earth were as tin-eared as the Earth people, not knowing high music when they heard it. And there was high music in the offing.

The actual sound that they first heard seemed like the distant screaming of wild horses.

"It must be a forest fire," said Charles, "and all the horses are being burned to death. Let's get knives and go out. Horses are good to eat. We can cut pieces off them and they'll be already cooked.''

''It's music!'' said Helen with a happy lilt. Her virginal ears had never been much affected by Earth sounds, and now she knew the real thing when she heard it.

Closer now, it was a man (who must have been trying to save the wild horses) chanting the strong song from the middle of the noise—unless one wished to believe that it was the wild horses themselves singing the tune:

> *"I had a wife I loved galore,*
> *My blessed, brindled, blond Cobina,*
> *Until my flute went out the door,*
> *And out of bed my concertina."*

''Those aren't horse noises at all,'' Peter cried. ''They're sheep, and he's the docker cutting off their tails. Sheep make a lot of fuss when you dock them, and the docker is singing a song to amuse them.''

Then the second wave of it swept still higher:

> *"I played the fiddle and the fife,*
> *The harpsichord and hootie-hoosic,*
> *But bled inside to hear my wife:*
> *'It's loud enough, but is it music?'"*

''It's a slyclone,'' said Dorothy. ''It's blowing around and breaking the trees off, and that's what part of the noise is. And a man is singing for the slyclone to bring his house back.''

For a man was singing yet higher and stronger and woollier:

> *"I had a cow, I had a calf,*

100

I had a pig, I had a pony.
I killed them all when they did laugh
And called my carols caco-phony."

"It's a Gypsy funeral," said John. "They sing like that to scare the Devil away."

"But it's wonderful," Helen squealed, "wonderful! Open up your ears and hear all that jumping air."

Wonderful or not, it was nearer, and solid movement could be seen inside that approaching cloud of dust. The man, if he were a man, was singing still more strongly out of that cloud of dust and noise:

"My daughter was my pride of life,
But at my tunes she was a scoffer.
I took the blinking butcher knife
And sheared the erring ears right off her."

This was the strong happy stuff like they sang at weddings and funerals and massacres. They were the real tunes that the off-Earth horn had always sounded silently to them, and the grins it always brought to every Puca face were being grinned now—six happy, devil grins, seven if you count Bad John's. The tune plucked at their heartstrings, and Puca heartstrings are made from gusunka guts.

Woops, here comes another verse, higher and headier:

"I had a dog who when I played
He cringed himself and whined and howled him.
I went for him with spit and spade
And cut him up and disembow'led him."

"Oh rapture!" cried Helen. "There can't be any happier music than that. It would set the very frogs to dancing.''

"Oh rupture!" cried Peter. "It's moving. It's on wheels!"

Well, the Devil himself is on wheels, according to Puca fables. He's a mechanical thing that got out of hand. And this thing, moving in the middle of a cloud of dust or wild horses, was on four bicycle or cart wheels. It was coming through the chosky bottoms, and in even a short dry spell those bottoms get pretty dusty. The thing was perched above the wheels like a crazy cat-castle of shining silver and gold, or of brass and chrome. The castle itself, intricate with instruments, was making an awful noise, and the man sitting in the castle was singing the wonderful verses:

> *"I showered riches on my wife*
> *And lived myself in durance frugal;*
> *But she's a fault that cost her life:*
> *She chattered while I played the bugle."*

Listen everybody, it's coming closer and getting better. Going to have to take the very sky off to get the full tone of it:

> *"My daughter never lived to wed*
> *For all my songs she'd sore berate them.*
> *I cut the eyeballs from her head*
> *And marinated them and ate them."*

Those are the high big songs, the kind of songs the Blessed sing in Heaven, real strong stuff in them.

He was a man all right, and he pedaled a four-wheeled cart that had a piano on it, and a big set of drums, and

French horns and that other kind of horns. Listen, there were drums on top of drums and horns growing out of horns! It bristled like a hedgehog with all the instruments. The man had a guitar and ukelele and a banjo slung around his neck, and a fiddle stuck under his chin. He was a slew-footed red-necked singing man, but not one of your Earthmen. You ever hear one of them sing like this?

> *"I had a child, I had a wife,*
> *I gave them all the pleasures due them;*
> *Until one night with knout and knife*
> *I fell upon them both and slew them."*

The man came to a stop in front of the Dulantys, and almost at once they began to know who he was. For one thing he was a Puca; he wasn't one of those shriveled little people they have around here. Then he gave them one last soaring verse which in its words partly explains why Puca song is so free and untrammeled, and which finds echoing accord in unsuspected places:

> *"No longer am I dim of brow,*
> *No longer am I wan and harried,*
> *Nor even critics irk me now,*
> *They all of them are dead and buried."*

"Pandemonium John!" the Dulantys cried in seven voices together.

And everybody knows who Pandemonium John is.

John Pandemonium was a high *Eigeas-Amhranai*—beyond anything that Earth people know. Take Homer and Dante and Benny B-Flat and the singer of the Elder Edda and mix them together, and you have only a hint of it. Dig up Bill the Bard and teach him to whistle, and add him in; catch an old-time coon-shouter, and a trumpet player born only yesterday, and the author of the Psalms; and Pindar with his lyre for the string section, and a bunch of kraut-head symphony-smiths; and the daughter of a hurdy-gurdy who has learned opera, and a red-clay-country fiddler; add them together. You're not coming close yet, but you're getting the idea.

A music critic of the planet of the Cameroi once wrote that the music and song of the Puca, compared even to that of Earth, was simplistic, childish, monstrous, grotesque, and monotonous. But that planet-name-dropping music critic himself had a tin ear, to write so mistakenly of the music of the golden-eared Pucas.

Pandemonium John was a Puca like the Dulantys, but he had been too old when he came to Earth to learn the trick of looking like an Earth person. If the Puca look funny to Earth people, well, Pandemonium John looked funny even to other Pucas. He had the pug and the mug to excess. He was lean and crestfallen as a winter crow, and he walked with a dangerous swooping motion as though he were standing up in a rowboat.

As a high master of the Bagarthach, John Pandemonium was supposed to be a pangnostic, one who knew everything. He was supposed to be, but he had the appearance of a rather simpleminded fellow—except for his one great talent. Pandemonium had had a wife and daughter of the Earth people. This should have given him great opportunity to observe custom. There had been difficulties, however. Many of his verses referred to the inability of his wife and daughter to adjust to him. There was nothing allegorical or symbolic about these pieces. Symbolism and allegory do not pertain to the Pucas. They were all literal accounts of literal happenings.

● ● ●

The Dulanty kids and Pandemonium John rigged planks and rolled the pandemonium (that was the name of the fantastic rolling castle of musical instruments) onto the deck of the *Sea Bear* which was bigger and better bottomed (though less elegant) than the *Ile*. Pandemonium John accepted their homage. He told them that he had received a flying Bagarthach that all was not right with their clan. He had come to check on them and their parents.

"I have exchanged Bagarthachs at a distance with your parents," Pandemonium said when he had made himself comfortable in the deck officer's chair. "Frank tells me in verse that it is a race: which will kill him first, the Sickness, or the alien creatures who look like people. Henry is mildly defiant in his incarceration, but of course he does not have any hope of living to be an old man. Witchy is sometimes in a state where she confuses essence with accidence. The Earth people have a humorous name for the state—insanity. Crossing the line for her won't be very difficult or very sudden. She'll be dead in about a week. I have already communicated with Veronica, dead and buried, but not so long dead and buried that she cannot receive and send back Bagarthachs. She says for you all to do whatever must be done at any moment, and she says that you will always know what to do. So your parents are either all dead, or doomed to a quick death."

"That is all right," Elizabeth said, "it saves us the trouble."

"Oh, oh!" Helen cried in alarm. "The advice! It's coming. I can hear it rumbling up out of Pandemonium's paunch already. Take cover, everybody."

"There is no reason to take cover from any advice of mine," John Pandemonium said. "There is no reason, really, for any Puca ever to take cover from anything. You do not take cover from rain or sleet as Earthmen do, do you? Rather you soak in them and luxuriate in them. So let it be with my words, let them rain on you!

"There is an Earth proverb, 'If you can't be good, be careful.' Defy this word; it is the adage of the scowling devil. There is another Earth proverb of a later and freer vintage, 'If you can't be careful, be good.' The latter is an improvement on the former, but avoid it also; it is the adage of the smiling devil. As Pucas, you do not have to be either good or careful. The one is a concept of Earth, the other of Hell. All you have to be is Pucas. Peoples on a dozen different worlds say that they are the lords of creation. We Puca do not know whether we are or not, but we decided a long time ago to act as though we were. Then what happens?"

"They knock our heads off every time." Helen said simply.

"Right," Pandemonium agreed, "they knock our heads off every time. Well we can grow new heads, in a manner of speaking. You children are the new heads. Grow like grass! Know every trick! Be direct in your dealings with the natives! You can always mop the blood up later. Be kindly and loving to all; and remember that whether we are the lords or not, we will act as though we were. It is better to play a joke on someone else than to have one played on you. We've played such jokes on several worlds, you know, that had people wiser and stronger and more numerous than ourselves, and (it is not necessary to add) better looking. On Earth, the conditions are much more favorable than in many other places. Though the Earth people are incomparably savage, they aren't very smart."

"And now, off with the formalities, and on with the levity," Helen said, and they got ready to have them-

106

selves a ball.

Pandemonium John had been traveling about Earth for years, examining situations and learning customs; and supporting himself by his (to Earth ears) unsupportable music. He worked his music-making in reverse, as a big sign on his pandemonium proclaimed:

> *"I'll play the horn all night and day,*
> *I'll play the drum around your city.*
> *The only time I'll go away*
> *Is when there's money in my kitty."*

Pandemonium made his living getting run out of towns. People would take up collections and pay him to leave with his, as they said, damnable music—a sad commentary on Earth culture.

Pandemonium had been arrested often, and once he had been investigated thoroughly. It was charged then that he was a spy for a foreign power, and that his pandemonium was actually an electronic transmitting instrument.

They took it apart piece by piece, measured, photographed, and X-rayed every fragment of it, and then put it together perfectly. They said that they were sorry, that they had been victimized by a crackpot who was probably a fascist and who saw subversives under every cubile.

Well, the pot had not been cracked, but the careful investigators had been. Pandemonium John *was* a spy for a foreign power, and his pandemonium *was* actually a transmitting instrument, though not an electronic one. Puca communication is based on cosmic resonance rather than on the electromagnetic bit, and the pandemonium contained a resonator by which Pandemonium could communicate with his home world.

But now Pandemonium was old and tired and racked

with Earth Allergy.

"I just can't cover all the ground myself any more," he said. "There are towns in my nine-state area that haven't heard the shrill of my pandemonium for twenty years. There are fair-sized hamlets that I never have been run out of. If only I had a partner! But nobody is interested."

"I'm interested," Charles said.

They talked about it then—while the rest of the kids were setting up a honkeroo with the various instruments—how it wouldn't have to be a grand thing like this first pandemonium, but a simple aggregation of no more than forty or fifty instruments. Pandemonium said that he would help Charles build it, that he would divide the territory with him and license him, and that Charles could pay him one third royalty—or cheat him out of it if he grew up to be a true Puca.

After that, the ice having been broken, they all threw a concert. Pucas can play instinctively any instrument whether they have ever seen it before or not. These were Puca instruments, though, for the purpose of deception, they had Earth shapes. And there was something special about several of the instruments—they were made of brass from the Puca home world. Puca brass and Earth brass, though chemically and metallurgically they may seem the same in their alloy, do not have the same tone.

The horns reached high and the strings unhitched all Earth inhibitions; the percussions really set it to rolling. Pandemonium John sang them hundreds of tunes from back home, putting Earth-English words to them as he went along. Then he gave them tunes in Puca and in High Puca. People, you do not hear something like that every day! They built whole mountains of Bagarthach verses until the music was jammed up solid as high as the trees.

Pandemonium drank half the barrel of choc beer, and

then it was afternoon and evening. The honkeroo lasted the rest of the day and well into the night. The Dulantys were supposed to be in hiding, of course, and for all they knew there were search parties out for them that very afternoon. But Pucas, if they start being careful, will be no Pucas at all.

They even gave Earth a go. Earth isn't as barren as you'd imagine. Though Earth symphonies and concerts and operas were laughable, yet there was the beginning of real boondock music on Earth. Pay the pitiful piper his penny, he has it coming.

They ran through a dozen of the great songs of Earth, *Birmingham Jail Blues, Take Me Back to Tulsa I'm Too Young to Marry, Shotgun Boogie, Red River Valley*, and *Rang-Dang-Doo*, disdaining lesser tunes.

And after a very long time the honkeroo broke up and they all went to bed, Pandemonium John spending the night with them.

But Charles did not sleep at once. He lit a small candle and leaned on one elbow and sketched. He was designing his own pandemonium.

"Peter!" he cried out suddenly, "could you design me a gear case that will play *The Old Apple Tree in the Orchard* at normal speeds and *Bell-Bottomed Trousers* when accelerated? And musical sails to go on one of the rafts? I'm thinking of a seagoing pandemonium."

"Sure, I'll do it in the morning," Peter said. Peter was a better mechanic than Charles.

At the same time, two sisters were taunting each other with Bagarthach verses in a new and more authentic beat. Elizabeth sang one.

• • •

"I had a little sister dear
As pretty as a springtime crocus.
I buried her without a tear,
She was a little too pre-co-cus."

Then Helen ground one out in fury:

"I also had a sister sweet,
I worshiped her, I idolized her,
Until I put her on to heat,
And accidentally vaporized her."

11

They Found a Hold More Near Their Blood

Marshall, the prosecutor, came and talked to Henry Dulanty in his cell, it not being a well-run jail.

"I like to come to the point," Marshall said. "You're a dead man, Dulanty. Man, Hell! I consider you an animal, and I'll kill you for one."

"Do you kill all animals?" Henry asked. "And why do you say 'You're a dead man,' then?"

"I kill all animals that look too much like men. You're a masquerading ape to me. But I'm curious. What are you? As to species, I mean."

"*Homo Pucalis*—that is, Puca Man," Henry told him.

"Puca man. Goblin man. So there really is such a thing—from somewhere. I'm familiar with the hoax or prank. It was only two years ago, and the journals are still looking for the answer. The case with the specimen in it appeared in the Anthropological Museum one afternoon; it was just as the lecture-guide with some very important people in tow came to that point. The case was there where there hadn't been a case before. The specimen inside was something that nobody had ever seen—something like you. And it was labeled Puca Man. Some jokers must have brought the whole thing in and set it up in short minutes."

"In short seconds," Henry said. "I was one of the jokers, and we had to work fast. It was a kinsman of mine who had died, and we considered it a rather good-natured prank to intrude him there. We have more fun at our burials and disposals than you do, and he had suggested it himself just before he died. And it *did* complete the collection. We placed it just beyond the effigy of Modern Man—the Puca, last and highest of the line."

"It somewhat resembled the Neanderthal, which somewhat resembles the ape," Marshall said.

"Both parts true," Henry agreed. "We've been here before, Marshall, and we may have been the Neanderthals. Much of our early history is unrecorded, or to be found only in the archaeology of alien worlds. A few of us have always been on Earth. Soon we'll become effective. We are small in numbers even on our home world; and there are never more than a few hundred of us on any world that we control. It is therefore necessary that we become the dominant elite, or perish. To become so we often have to be what would seem crude or cruel."

"You'll not become dominant here. We'll kill you off like the damned dragons you are."

"Yes, I begin to think that you will. But you won't win by it. We've laid dragons' eggs behind us. They're hatched and going now. You'll not know the young while they're growing. They are a time bomb in you. Which of us is the more primitive people is not the question. We are the more fluid, and therefore we will dominate. If we have to alter the world to our way, we will do it."

"You bugger, you're wrong!" Marshall said. "There was never a more fluid man than myself, and I make a one-man elite whatever I do. I'm a woollier man than any masquerading ape. I'll tell you about it, and then I'll taunt you, and very soon I'll kill you. I'm not giving you a handle to grab me by. You'll be dead before you can think of a way to use the information.''

"So will you also be dead, Marshall, before you use the information I gave you as to the Puca. You have only one thing on your mind, and you'll die with it still incompleted.''

"You fake, Dulanty. I'll tell my story nevertheless. I'm Mandrake Marshall, a local boy. Whenever I reach out my hand I do not bring it back empty. When I was seventeen years old I was a powerful boy, a complete illiterate, and I worked in the strip mines of Coalfactor Stutgard. I had not yet come to full life or consciousness.

"Then that man Stutgard became interested in the pitiful state of the football team at the little normal college he had attended. He sent me to college there, I was the best tackle they ever had; I played eight years. Eligibility was then an informal thing in the small teachers colleges.

"I had time on my hands at the college, Dulanty. One of the teachers, who had somewhere mastered those arts, offered to teach me to read and write. I learned the tricks pretty well in a month—the only real schooling I ever took under a teacher. But I had caught the sickness of ambition. I read considerable in those eight years, when I was not goofing off in the College Inn, or playing football. I have total recall. I remember and understand everything I have ever read. There is very little about History or Philosophy or Philology or Economics or the Beautiful Letters that I do not know. I have a contempt for the tone of this knowledge, but I needed the repertoire.''

This Mandrake Marshall was very big. Henry Dulanty measured him with his eye and judgment, and was unable to decide which of them was the larger.

"After those happy days, I was selected to go to the state legislature by the men who believed themselves to be

113

my masters," Marshall continued. "I was made house whip. I was the biggest man there, and I had the loudest voice and the meanest disposition. I made them physically afraid of me. I passed many bills by terrorizing my fellow members. I do not always behave so suavely as I am doing now."

"This is suavity, you yokel?"

"You shouldn't have called me that, Dulanty. I'm trying you now in a court that doesn't go by that name, and your appeal has just been denied."

"I didn't make any," Henry said.

"You'll appeal to murky Heaven before I'm through with you," Mandrake jeered. "But you're done. I have already decided to be your *Atropos*. Can you field it?"

"The oldest and ugliest of the Fates. You would cut my thread? We will see. I have, as it happens, a much more interesting biography than you have. But you wouldn't care to hear it."

"Now, I wouldn't. Oh, it's finished with you, Dulanty; now let me finish my story. I spent four years in the legislature, and during those four years I studied law irregularly, and was admitted to the bar. I came here and was made prosecutor. That's been two years. Now I need a big case to bring me to wider attention. I don't know quite what angle I'll employ, but you are that case. Whichever form I cast the sequence in, I'll kill you in the grand manner."

"Is it ambition only, little Master Mandrake, or have you animosity towards me?" Henry asked.

"You're damned right I have animosity towards you, Dulanty, you ape! There is enmity between our flesh from the beginning. We fought before, in an ice cave a million years ago, either on Earth or off it. You're an almost-man. You'll find the hate stronger here in the sticks than you

114

would in a city. I won't have you on the same world with me! But how I will use you with the people here! You'll serve my future at the same time. I'll make them loathe you for a murdering ape, and love me as the beast killer. After all, you did murder our great noble first citizen of Lost Haven."

"This Stutgard, whom I *didn't* kill, was a pig."

"Sure he was, Dulanty, but he was my kind of pig. The men hated him while he was alive, and so did I. Never mind, the thing will work."

"Why did Stutgard let the town die, Marshall? I know minerals, and there's a lot left in Lost Haven."

"Since you'll soon be dead, and you say the same thing about me, there's no harm in telling you. If you know minerals, you know that coal is the cheapest of them all. Stutgard decided to mine gold instead of coal. To do this, it was necessary to shrink the population of the town and turn it into a shell. He dealt souls in the manner of Pavel Ivanovitch. You know Pavel?"

"I do. I begin to recognize the device."

"Some of Stutgard's dead souls are now in California and some in Texas; some of them are actually dead; and some of them never lived at all. Do you know the population of Lost Haven, Dulanty?"

"About three hundred persons, some seventy families, I believe."

"Ah, but that is only the apparent population. Do you know how many relief checks have been coming into Lost Haven every month? A little more than one thousand of them. Stutgard got the lion's share."

"And several of you got jackals' shares?"

"Some of us drew nice prebends and livings. Fifty family sustenance checks a month will keep a man like me in pocket money, though not, of course, satisfied."

"And one of the jackals (Crocker I guess him) got too greedy? Didn't you other jackals resent it? Yes, it had to be Crocker. Why not execute him properly for the murder, since he's guilty? He'd boggle his eyes and put on a good enough show."

"I don't want a show, I want a spectacle. I'll kill him later and in another fashion. You are what I need—a mad monster. Yes, I have me a real flesh and blood—or ichor and offal—monster to convict. How they'll blood-hate you! How they'll love me!"

"I smell more income than the bogus relief checks, Marshall, though that might run around sixty thousand dollars a month."

"You're smart, for an animal, Dulanty. Oh, there's the land in the pits, quite a few sections of it. Crop histories are easily created by a man who controls the men who pass on them. Stutgard got paid for not growing cotton on land that never saw cotton, and for corn where corn was a stranger. The land had always been worthless, except for the coal, and Stutgard had originally stolen most of it for a dollar an acre. I expect to inherit all this, but that's several steps ahead."

"What you want now is a man-kill, Marshall?"

"No. A monster-kill, Dulanty. You're the monster. Don't you get the message?"

Henry Dulanty grinned, and then he chanted in boyish sing-song:

> "Oh Mandrake man, of giants bred,
> You didn't guess one singing trifle
> Would ever enter in your head—
> A message from a talking rifle."

"What's with you, ape, chanting verses like a kid?"

Marshall demanded.

"You never met the Bagarthach verses during your encounter with the Beautiful Letters, Marshall?" Henry asked. "But the Bagarthach is handy. You can milk a cow with it, or charge a battery, or kill a man—as I have just done. What other literary form serves so well? But I may cheat you out of the monster-kill, Marshall."

"You mean a break-out, Dulanty? I hope you try it. It'd satisfy me more, emotionally, to hunt you down. I'd have real blood out of you then, and not have to be satisfied with the burning."

"The bulls have pawed the ground long enough, Marshall. It is time for the weaker one to grow too nervous, and to lunge. Two worlds have met here this afternoon in our persons. Our talk seemed trivial, but it was key stuff. We could not strike a modus. Now we go to war, each world in its own fashion. You outnumber us here a hundred million to one, but as a betting man I don't know which I'd take. Get out of my cell now, Marshall! Get out, you crud! Move when I tell you to move!"

"You're in no position to tell anyone to get out, Dulanty. You're the prisoner here. I'm as big as you, and that's big. I've taken a hundred men tougher than any you've ever seen, and I've never been taken. I mean it when I say that I don't believe there's a man in the world can take me."

"But you don't call me a man. Have at an animal then! That toy won't stop me, Marshall."

The bulls had pawed the ground long enough. The weaker bull broke and lunged. Marshall lunged at Dulanty with a sap in his hand, hit big Henry with it but hit him badly, and it didn't drop him. Then Henry closed before Marshall could swing a second time.

It went hot and heavy. It was, of course, a war of the

Worlds. Travelers not known to Earthmen have argued over various pairs, which could win in a showdown: a Ganymede Agriothere or a Stentor Phoneus; an Arcturus Four Fanger or a Tankersly Tiger; a Puca or an Earthman (assuming both to be prime fighting specimens). The Earthmen were known to be very uneven in their abilities, but it was thought that the most competent among them were pretty horny.

Ah, they settled it: a Puca can whip an Earthmen, both of them being prime specimens. Marshall would never think to call for help, but it was near and it came to the roaring action.

When they got Marshall out of the cell his clothes were mostly torn off. His face was broken, and he blew blood-bubbles from mouth and ear with every heavy breath. But he was a man who'd fight a panther or a Puca. He was laughing!

They had to support him on his feet, but he was laughing.

"Wish I could have stayed for more, Dulanty," he said. "I'm still not convinced you can take me that way, but you did make me look bad for a minute. You'd have killed me, and I hardly noticed, it was so much fun. But I can take you more ways than you'd imagine, and you've multiplied my coming pleasure by this antic."

12

A Mountainful of Murdered Indians

Fulbert Fronsac and a lawyer came to see the children. The lawyer does not want his name used. He is still practicing law in T-Town, and he does not consider his part in this case a successful one.

The children scanned their coming from a long way off with three or four senses. They would not be slipped up on again by anyone. But Catherine de Medici was lively with recognition, so the children knew that it was Fulbert coming with someone who might almost be trusted.

Trusted maybe, but put on the defensive at the start. They could see that man with Fulbert now and they knew what he was. With one of them, you state your maximum claim first. You can give ground gracefully later if you've got more of that ground grabbed off.

"You'll never get the *Ile* back, you old Fulbert you!" Helen called out in a ringing voice while the two men were still some distance off, "and that crooked lawyer can't help you get it. We got an instrument signed by yourself for a start, and a start is all we need."

"That lawyer'd have to get a writ and a mandamus and all that stuff," Peter challenged. "And we'd all lie and stick together on it and make holographic depositions and holler persecution. We'd make you wish you'd never taken this case, you lawyer.''

"I've not come for the *Ile*," Fulbert said when he was nearer, "except for a sentimental visit of a few minutes. Yes, this gentleman is a lawyer, but I don't know how Helen and Peter recognized him as one.''

"How did you, Helen?'' the lawyer asked.

"Oh, when we were little our folks taught us to recognize simple objects,'' Helen said. "Like you say—'That is a stone—that is a horse—that is an Osage orange tree—that is a road apple—that is a lawyer.' What does he look like to you, Fulbert, a humpbacked Jersey cow?''

"Your logic is perfect until it turns the corner, little girl,'' the lawyer said. "Do you discern me as to subspecies?''

"Sure, you're a T-Town lawyer,'' Peter cut in.

"We could modify it in more detail, but you'd probably take offense,'' Helen said.

We don't say that the Dulanty children did not have preternatural powers. In some things they seemed to have, but there was nothing preternatural about this. About two weeks before this, about a week before the Dulantys' real troubles began, that lawyer had been in Lost Haven. "That man over there is a lawyer for T-Town,'' Henry Dulanty had said to his brother Frank (and Helen and Peter had been present). "I may get him to check a few titles and quitclaim deeds,'' Henry had added to Frank, "it's impossible that there's a legal basis for everything that's going on in Lost Haven.''

You hear something like that and you remember it. And you work it in lefthandedly when the time comes, and you score an early point.

"I am counsel for your father-and-uncle Henry Dulanty,'' the lawyer said to the children. "I believe, from some things that Mr. Fronsac here has told me, that you

120

have information that may save Henry's life. But it is in such an odd form that we will have to extract it carefully, and then perhaps it will give us corroborative proof."

"He means," said Fulbert, "that your information may point to fuller proof which—"

"Please," said Helen, "it is boorish to talk down to people. Now then, gentleman, you just come with me to the captain's wardroom, and do not pay any attention to these little children here. I will have one of my girls make tea, and afterwards I will give you all the information which I believe it is wise for you to have. This way, please, onto our flagship."

Helen was smart there. She knew that if two grown men got into the boathouse of the *Ile*, there would just barely room left for her to squeeze in, and no room for the other children.

But Fulbert knew the limitations of the *Ile*, so he arranged for the parliament to be held on the deck of the roomier *Sea Bear*. All the other children gathered there too, except Dorothy who stayed on the *Ile* to make tea.

"Now then," the lawyer said, "let's get on with what you all saw the night Mr. Stutgard was killed."

"Please!" said Helen. "In the best society, one first speaks at length of everything else except the subject directly on the mind. Then, when the subject does come up, it is as though it came up quite by accident."

"Oh great green grapefruit!" swore the lawyer who was a pious man. But he sighed and made the effort.

"That's a queer-looking little mountain there," he offered.

"We love it!" Helen sparkled. "It's full of murdered Indians."

"How do you mean, full of them?"

"Full up full solid with them, is what I mean," Helen

121

said. "I estimate there's about thirty thousand of them in it, figuring cubic capacity and the settling of the mass through the centuries, and the coefficient of traverse lay (the old bodies aren't stacked in as neatly as they might be), and deducting for the tunnels and big rooms and lounges that are inside the mound. I believe that the last Indians buried there were the Caddos, about the time of the breakup of their confederation. Phoebe Jane says that the Shawnees were the last ones buried there, but that is impossible. One of the old dead Indians I talked to in the mound agrees that it's impossible. He says that he never saw those Johnny-come-lately Shawnees in his life, or since. It's only a hundred and fifty years since the Shawnees came into this part of the country. Phoebe is wrong. Did you know that the Indians today are woefully ignorant of Indian history?''

"No, I didn't know that," the lawyer said.

Then they talked about the blackberries, that it should be a good crop next year; about the plenitude of fine fish still in the rivers in spite of the depredations of the Fabers and other evil folk; about how will you know how long to milk a goat, and when it is time to breed her again, and is that what is making Catherine de Medici so cranky that you can hardly say a word to her without her flying off the handle?

In this manner Helen skillfully steered the conversation into every sort of channel, until Dorothy sounded the old squeeze-bulb automobile horn that was the distress signal on the *Ile de France*.

"Go see what is the matter, John," said Helen. "And if Peter or Charles or Elizabeth has set something afoot through misguided humor, I will settle with them later."

"Dorothy can create her own situations," Peter said.

"These children are sometimes almost more than I can

manage," Helen complained to the men. And something in the corner of the lawyer's mind was nudging his main mind. "She *is* the youngest of them just as she is the smallest, isn't she?" the thing in the corner of his mind asked. "She *is* only six years old, isn't she? You saw the papers that were drawn up to commit the bunch of them to a home if they should ever be found."

John had gone on board the *Ile*, and he was back almost immediately.

"Dorothy built the fire too big and it caught the curtains," John said. "She's afraid it will set fire to the whole boat unless we put some water on it."

"Well, why doesn't she—why don't you both put water on it?" Helen asked patiently.

"She says that if she uses the drinking water to put out the fire, then she'll have to use river water to make the tea, and she's afraid our guests will notice that it tastes rotten."

"Tell her to use river water to put out the fire, and the drinking water to make tea," Helen settled it. "And you help her, John."

Once more they talked about everything, as why are crows' eggs smaller than hens' eggs, and then a crow will grow bigger than a chicken will. But almost immediately John came back to them with more bad news from the *Ile*.

"Dorothy says that she doesn't remember how to make tea," he announced. "She just remembered that she never did know how. She never made tea in her life. She says will onion soup do just as good? She remembers part of the way you make onion soup."

"I must do everything," said Helen, "everything." But she left the parliament on the *Sea Bear* and went onto the *Ile* to make tea.

All this time the lawyer had been having, down in a

left-hand corner of his mind, a waking dream. He was an intelligent man—though he doesn't always seem so here in an unusual environment—and he was accustomed to analyze. He knew quite a bit about weighing evidence. He would weigh the evidence brought to him by his waking dream.

The dream was that the voices of the children did not always accord with their expressions or with the movements of their lips and throats. Often a child would say half a dozen words clearly before he began to move his lips; indeed, it seemed that he moved his lips only when he remembered that he should not be caught talking without the outward sign. And sometimes the lip movement would come like an afterthought when the spoken phrase had already been completed.

Again, one of the small speakers would be just a little out of phase, or would speak loudly and clearly with no lip or throat movement at all, like a ventriloquist when the lawyer was not looking directly at him, or usually her.

"They don't speak as other persons do," the dream hinted to the lawyer. "They think out loud when they wish to do so, and vocal cords (if such they have) have nothing to do with it. And then—as they almost always remember to do—they fake the appearance of regular speech."

And there was another thing running through that waking dream of the lawyer. Out of the corner of his eye he seemed to see, for instance, a veritable gargoyle—incredible in ear and crine and scruff, nightmarish in lip and snout, bulbous and cubistic-futurist in eye. But the lawyer would look directly at the place where the gargoyle had been detected, and would see one of the children—rather funny-looking in the case of several of them, but not a gargoyle, not a monster. And then the lawyer would almost—but not quite—catch another of them in the

124

strange act of metamorphosis.

These were odd things to dream of those chattering children, especially when one was nine parts awake. And it was an even odder recognition that went through his mind: "These are Poltergeister made visible."

Enough of that; he tried to rouse himself to fuller wakefulness, but he had been quite wide awake.

"You'd better start the questioning now," Charles told the lawyer. "You'll never get it over with if Helen's in it."

"Briefly then," said the lawyer, "Henry Dulanty, the father of some of you and the uncle of the rest, goes on trial tomorrow for the murder of Mr. Stutgard. Due to—ah—a peculiarity of appearance and manner that Henry shares with the rest of you, it is pretty certain that prejudice will find him guilty. A hate show is scheduled, and it will take honest evidence clearly presented to offset this.

"Mr. Fronsac says that you as a group have information that will prove Henry innocent and another man guilty, but that the information is in a strange form. But if you will tell me what really happened and who is guilty, then we will know where we are. Now then, do you really know who killed Mr. Stutgard?"

"Yes. It was Mr. Crocker," Peter said.

"Did one of you actually see it done?"

"Yes, Bad John here saw it all."

"Did you see it clearly, John?" the lawyer asked John.

"No. I didn't see it at all," John said. "I didn't see Mr. Crocker there. He must have left just as I climbed up to the window. The door was still moving shut as if someone had just left the room. But I saw Mr. Stutgard, and the blood was still thumping out of him in thumps."

"But your brother Peter just said that you actually saw it all."

"No. He said that Bad John saw it all. I'm John, not Bad John. This is Bad John beside me here, the one that looks just like me only dirtier and scrawnier."

"Ah yes. I see, but not with eyes. Bad John is the ghost child?"

"Don't you dare call him that, you itchy-nosed lawyer!" Elizabeth said. "He's no more a ghost than you are. He's scaredest of all of us of ghosts because he can see them oftenest, and they can punch him like they can't do it to us. Bad John is just different because he died when he was a baby. A lot of people are different from other people."

"I agree with you there, Elizabeth," the lawyer said. "Can Bad John hear me talking?"

"Of course he can," Peter said. "There's nothing the matter with his ears. If you can't hear him, you're the one there's something the matter with."

"I'm sorry that I can't hear you, Bad John," the lawyer said. "Things would be simpler if I could, if everybody could. Going into court with an unbodied voice would be fantastic; but when that voice is mute to all except the elect, that tastes of madness. Mr. Fronsac here has given me a statement; he says he will go into court with it and swear that he has heard Bad John and that the account was given him by Bad John. But would Mr. Fronsac be believed?"

"I sure do doubt it," Elizabeth said. "Everybody knows that he's the worst liar in Lost Haven."

Helen came back with happy green fire in her eyes, and with the tea in glasses on an old plank board for a tray. The lawyer and Fronsac each took one at the same instant, and burned themselves howlingly.

"*Judas Prêtre!*" Fronsac swore. He, of all Earthmen, should have known better. He was familiar with this

126

bunch. And the glasses were so hot as to be almost incandescent.

"Ung ung ung hoo hoo!" the lawyer moaned.

"I always wanted to find someone dumb enough to do that to," Helen chortled. "Burned the living fingers off you, didn't it? I wanted to see if you were paying attention, and you weren't. The ambient heat should have warned you when your hands were still a half inch from the glasses. Lemon or persimmon with your tea?"

"Persimmon," said Fulbert sadly, for he had been over this road before.

"Why, lemon, Helen, please," the lawyer said.

"What a rude thing to say!" Helen exploded. "How would people who live on rafts have lemons? You could have spared my feelings at least. How'd you get to be a lawyer if you don't understand people any better than that?"

"Ah, persimmon then," said the lawyer "or anything, even koneion."

You think that stopped Helen? Nobody can know it all; but if you have a cousin like Peter who can send you the answers silently, then you're hard to stop. He sent it, and she caught it with a flick of her head.

"You lead a Socrates, and I'll see you with the koneion," she bantered the lawyer. "We'd do him in all over again, the silly fruit. And just how sure are you that it isn't hemlock I've given you?"

After it had cooled a little, the lawyer and Fronsac drank the tea with persimmon squeezings. The taste startled them. It was a new thing. Indeed, those persons who commonly take tea with persimmon—and there are fewer than two of them in the world—uniformly agree that there is no drink like it.

"I assume that you have been asking questions in my

absence," Helen said when they had drunk together enough to satisfy the rite, "and I assume that the questioning has been fruitless. Where are we?"

"I have covered part of the ground with the other children," the lawyer said, "but I have missed the salient point, if there is one."

"I guess an axe is about as salient a point as there is, in the true meaning of the words," Helen offered. "Let's talk about axes."

"All right," the lawyer said. "Yes, there is some confusion there. A small axe, a child's axe was found in the room. It was honed as sharp as a razor and had no mark on it. It could not have done the job, the blade being not a quarter the length of those long wounds. It was as though the small axe was left as an indication that the murder was committed with an axe, but not with that one. It was a sort of a signature. Can any of you tell me about it?"

"It was my axe. I left it there," John said. "I was scared when I saw that Mr. Stutgard was axed. I bolted out the window and left my axe behind me."

"Did you come out of the window empty-handed, John?"

"No. I picked up the big axe with the blood and the hand smudges on it and brought it along instead. I thought that it seemed a lot heavier. I was mixed up for a minute there."

"Lightning just struck," the lawyer said. "Where's the big axe now?"

"Silly Elizabeth put it in a potato sack and hid it," Helen said bitterly. "She said she would keep it back till it seemed like the right moment to tell about it. A whole ocean went by her while she was waiting for just one bucket of water to come along. If I'd had it, I'd have transmitted the prints and had this case wrapped up three

128

days ago.''

''And Helen would have got herself killed, and worse, us,'' Elizabeth protested. ''The axe is available and in good condition, though it's begun to rust around the edge of the blood. We were careful not to smudge it, and all the marks on it are Crocker's. And it's got the big C burned into the haft. Everybody in Lost Haven would recognize it as Crocker's axe.''

''Why would Crocker have left such a damaging thing behind him?'' the lawyer wondered to them.

''Bad John's trying to tell you if you'd only listen,'' Peter said. ''He's saying that Mr. Crocker almost had a fit when he saw him in the room. They scared each other. Mr. Crocker was able to see Bad John then. A lot of people can't. But it startles a lot of people when they can see someone and see through him at the same time. Bad John said that Mr. Crocker jumped like he had seen a real ghost. He dropped the axe, or threw it at Bad John, and ran out of the room. Then John climbed up through the window and took Crocker's axe, so it wasn't there if Mr. Crocker came back looking for it.''

''We will certainly look into this aspect of the matter, and today,'' the lawyer said. (Elizabeth had told him where she had hidden the potato sack with the axe in it.) ''Ah—there is one other thing, children, that you might cast some light on before we leave you for a while. Three children of Lost Haven have been lost for two days. It is believed that they were playing along this stream, or looking for somebody here. They were probably looking for you for Crocker. You haven't seen any trace of them, have you? We don't want to complicate things with another happening.''

''We haven't seen any children,'' Dorothy said (with

Helen and Peter sending thought-waves at her like sledgehammers, "Shut your silly speech, let the ones with brains handle this!"), "but there were two big boys and one middle-sized boy who thought they had the hop on us. Helen honey-talked them till Charles got the jump on them with the big rifle. Then he marched them back in the woods and killed them and cut off their ears."

"What, what are you saying, little girl?" the lawyer asked boggle-eyed.

"Mere childhood fantasy," Fulbert cut in hastily. "Dorothy here has a vivid imagination. I have traded tall stories with her by the hour."

"Oh, ha, ha, of course," the lawyer agreed. "I don't know what makes me so jumpy. Imagine me entertaining the thought that—"

"We'll leave you now, kids," Fulbert said. "Stay quiet and stay hidden. We see now that Crocker would kill you to shut you up. But don't worry. Remember, we're on your side."

"The most damnable equivocation I've ever heard," Helen muttered.

The lawyer was thoughtful as he walked back through the bottoms with Fronsac.

"That youngest girl, Helen, it is hard to believe that she is only six years old," he said, "though from appearance she would not even be that. She's as eerie as their Bad John, and as comical."

"Yes. But when I have left them, I always carry away the impression that it is they who are the real people, and that the real people are a little less," Fulbert said.

"Real people, Fronsac? Is there some doubt of it?"

"What do you think the ruckus is all about? You're a city man. The smalltowners can sense these things a little sharper. You've just had a brush with a multiplex alien mind. You've hardly noticed the effect yet, but you'll never be the same again.''

''They are so rapid and intelligent for their ages, that they might—ah—almost be dangerous,'' the lawyer said.

''Do you—ah—really believe so?'' Fulbert asked the lawyer with an odd twinkle.

Fulbert and the lawyer got the death axe from the potato sack where Elizabeth had hidden it. They saw that there were very good prints, both in blood and in excitement-staining sweat. They went to Frank Dulanty and talked with him. They all agreed that the Crocker case might be built solidly enough to overcome the animosity against Henry. After all, there was plenty of animosity against Crocker in Lost Haven also. A lot of evidence against Crocker quickly gathered itself.

They tapped four men of the town who said that they would testify on various aspects if a case could really be made against Crocker; but if a case could not be made, they would speak no word to their own injury. The lawyer convinced them that the case could be made.

The prints would tie Crocker to his axe, and the axe would tie itself to Stutgard's body and its clear hack marks. The lawyer knew prints. He telegraphed the index of these.

The news of a change in status travels rapidly. The tide had turned for Henry Dulanty, and all the creatures of that particular littoral knew it. Mandrake Marshall got the feel of it like a dismal but certain wave when he was off fishing at some distance. Earthmen are able to receive such pre-monitions in ways that other persons cannot understand. Marshall gathered up his gear at once and began his return to stop this nonsense. He knew that his very swift intervention was indeed to keep the plan from falling apart.

Crocker got the feel of the new situation when he was sitting at his supper—the meanest supper in town, though he was now the richest man in town. He got in his car and fled to Marshall for protection, knowing instinctively on what road to meet him. He fled to Marshall, who intended to kill him eventually, for protection against the new circumstance that threatened to kill him sooner.

Phoebe Jane Lanyard got the feel of it down in her shack in the strip pits. She had a very close feel for the whole Dulanty case.

Witchy got it in the ward in the hospital where she lived, and smiled in green-eyed benevolence like the good witch she was. Then she didn't smile any more, for a new premonition swept over her. She foresaw that the fortunate pendulum would swing back again, and like a scimitar.

But Henry Dulanty didn't feel it at all—the change in his own status. His Earth Sickness prevented him from receiving either Earth or Puca precognizance.

One of the jailers, who had hated Henry and been frightened of him, looked in at him kindly that evening. The jailer had received the psychic hint, and he had also overheard words about the thing. The monster already convicted would become a man cleared, and one to be neither feared nor hated.

"I never believed that you did it, Mr. Dulanty," that jailer said. "I always said that you were an honest and decent man. I guess that you will be leaving us pretty soon now."

"Who knows? My trial begins tomorrow," Henry said.

The jailer looked at Henry archly.

"There is some talk in the last several hours that there might not be any trial for *you,* Mr. Dulanty. In fact, I wouldn't be at all surprised if they came and got you out of jail before this night is over.

"Thank you for whatever you are trying to tell me," Henry said.

The jailer meant that he had heard and sensed that the finger was being put on Crocker now, and that Henry Dulanty would probably be released without more ado. But Earth Sickness had dulled Henry's intuition and communication. Had he been in his full powers he would have known more what the man meant than the man himself knew.

But Henry, in his stultification and listlessness, thought that the jailer was trying to say that lynchers were coming for him that night.

He decided to act now. He had already set up his pattern for it. Since he had been in, he had been very rambunctious and troublesome once or twice every twenty-four hours, and had followed every tirade with a long period of peacefulness.

He put on the show now. He shook the jail and shouted himself hoarse for half an hour. Then he subsided suddenly. They had grown to expect it of him.

"He'll be quiet for the rest of the night," the guards said.

There were two ways Henry Dulanty could get out of his cell. He could unlock the cell door with a Bagarthach, or with a key.

He raised his head, and the Bagarthach came to him in this form:

> *"Unlikely lock, unlucky lock,*
> *I'll batter you ka-zow ka-zammy*

The way the chopper chopped the block,
And bust you with a mummy-whammy!

It wasn't a very good Bagarthach. He felt like a silly kid making up a rime like that, and a Puca in his full powers cannot let himself feel foolish. A Bagarthach is not effective unless chanted with confidence and Henry had lost his. He doubted if the verse, recited in his present state of mind would cause the lock to fall apart.

The key had come to him in this manner:

One of Phoebe Jane's cousins, up for stealing three black calves (you'd have stolen them yourself if you'd seen how pretty they were), was a trusty in this very jail, he having been here before and knowing the folks.

Now, on his first coming to the jail, Henry had been curious when the jailer had locked him in.

"There are sixteen different cells, and only four different keys," he said to the jailer. "Why is that?"

"What's the matter with you?,' the jailer asked him. "There are sixteen different keys that I have on my ring there."

"No, there are only four different keys," Henry said.

One day, when Phoebe's cousin was shooting the moose with him through the door, Henry told him what to do.

"In the orderly room or somewhere accessible to you, you will know the place better than I do, there will be a board with duplicate keys to some of the cells hanging on it. Mine will not be there, since I am in for murder, but the keys for either cell seven or nine or thirteen should be there. Make a tracing of any of them, they are the same, and give it to Phoebe Jane the next time she comes. Also make a note of the thickness of the key. Tell her to have my brother Frank make a key like that."

It was done, and Frank Dulanty made the key and sent it back to the jail by Phoebe Jane, and her cousin passed it in to Henry. It was a stubby key so as not to be conspicuous, and with so short a cross-piece that only a person with great strength of thumb and finger (which Henry had) could make it work. But you can't make a very accurate key from a tracing.

It wasn't a very good key. It wasn't a very good Bagarthach. Henry recited the verse in a low voice and a half-hearted manner, and put the key in the old warded lock. It wasn't a very good lock either. Almost any verse or any key would have opened it.

At five minutes before nine o'clock, Henry Dulanty unlocked the door of his cell and walked out. The inmates had all been fed long before and were smoking in their bunks and listening to their radios. Henry passed as though invisible.

He met the jailer in a little closed corridor. The jailer was surprised to see Henry out of his cell.

"I haven't received any orders to release you *yet*, Mr. Dulanty," he said. "Did the sheriff or somebody else come with a writ to release you? I didn't see anybody come in. I'm sure it's all right, but I'd better go check. You might have to sign something before you go."

"I took the liberty to take my liberty," Henry said. "I will have to put you out of the way for a little while."

Henry clamped onto the jailer something that was very like the Japanese Sleep Hold. In fact it was the Puca Sleep Hold. He throttled the jailer very gently and stretched him out to sleep on the floor.

He lifted the block key and the passage key from the jailer's ring.

He left the jail sector, the building, and the town in quiet haste.

13

In Brazen Clash of Helm and Greave

When Mandrake Marshall and Sheriff Train arrived, it was too late. Dulanty had got away clean; and nobody knew in what direction, nor whether on foot or in car. But Marshall didn't waste too much time treating of the ineptitude of the jailers. The situation was made to order for him. The jailbreak was a break for him too.

He began to give orders, and he was good at it.

"Get on the air and put out an alert that the Mad Killer is loose, and to take him dead or alive before he kills again," Marshall ordered everybody.

"I am still the sheriff," Sheriff Train protested. "The man obviously feared a lynching, and with reason. There is now pretty clear evidence that he's innocent and that— ugh—Crocker is guilty."

"Shut up, Train!" Marshall snapped. "I don't want to hear any more about a case against Crocker. Shall I draw it out for you? It would be effective to make it that Dulanty killed the sheriff when he fled. Do you want me to stage that one? Dulanty has broken and fled. That's confession enough of guilt for anyone. And for his second crime he has left the jailer dying here on the floor. Unless you want to be the one dying on the floor, Train."

"But Sam is no more dying than you are," Sheriff

Train protested. "He's just a little scared and the wind squeezed out of him. He'll be able to walk home when he settles down a little."

"He shouldn't be walking at all," Marshall said evenly. "Damn you, Sam, do you want me to fix it so you can't walk at all? Make him lie down, Train. Lie down, damn you, Sam! I'm calling the tune here. Ring for the wagon and get poor Sam here to the hospital. And if anyone asks, he's at the point of death."

"Marshall, I'm not going to let you tear up the whole region and kill an innocent man with one of your manhunts," Sheriff Train insisted.

Marshall felled Train with an openhanded blow that would have killed a colt, stunned him stupid, picked him up and shook the remaining manhood out of him; then he flung him into a corner.

"A few of the boys will be in," Marshall said to Train who was now no more than a lump on hands and knees. "Deputize them without any delay or I'll kill you."

And Train would do it. Marshall had a little private army of about twenty men, ready to be deputized any time an unauthorized cock crowed. Most of them were already on the move.

Then Marshall quickly set the affair going with his broadcasts and his hot-line phone calls. He knew that many of the men in that country loved a manhunt. They were night hunters by instinct. Then Marshall left the jail, picked up Crocker where he had cached him, collected the hounds, and started on the live hunt.

"He isn't armed, Crocker," Marshall said. (They were hunting cronies now, though they both understood that one of them would eventually have to kill the other by their ethic.) "The jailer was armed, and Dulanty didn't even lift it off of him when he laid him out. That makes it

138

mighty handy for me, because I did lift it off of him. And the Dulanty didn't go by car. None's been stolen. There were no confederates around; there never have been any. The brother is still with the T-Town lawyer and the drunk in Lost Haven. We'd better get him too, though. You're his patsy, from the comical stories I hear. I don't want that other Dulanty killing you before I get around to it. You were my patsy first.

"I'll put out another alert that the Mad Brother is on his way to meet the Mad Killer, and that both are armed and deadly. I'll get the whole brood."

Marshall's car was a regular command-station with transmitter and phones.

"There's a roadblock on everything down to a cow-path," Marshall said after he'd put out the latest alert, "and Henry bedamned Dulanty doesn't know this country except just around Lost Haven. I think he's headed for his wife at old Wan-Wit on the Neosho, and he's got to cross plenty of roads to get there. I've got it all planned out. It'll be better than a bear-kill."

"What's to plan out?" Crocker asked sulkily. "It's just to catch him and kill him and plant the jailer's gun in his hand, with a couple of shots fired from it."

"Where's the artist in you, Crocker? Must you always be the philistine? We need climax and agony, and a strong and legal swashbuckler (me) standing boot-deep in brains and gore. One shot won't stop him, Crocker, not if I get him just in the flank. The next one won't quite drop him either if I can put it where I want to, but it'll hurt him bad. And then a little gut-shot rather riles up a bear, or the bear in a man. There's a lot of bear in him, you know. I like to see one of them gnash.

"He'll keep coming after I put eight or nine shots into him, Crocker. I believe I can put them just where I want

139

them. I'm the best shot in this country, and I know my anatomy. And he'll still be able to talk, or at least to hear me, after he's stretched out at full length—if monsters do uncoil to full length when they come to die. What do you think he'll say when I put the gun to his head, and him too blood-spent to move? Will he beg, do you think?''

"No, Marshall, that man won't beg. You wouldn't want him to. It'd spoil a good hunt. But he'd bite through a boot you set to his mouth. I'm a better artist than you, though. You should bring in the blood-animals to kill an animal. There's nothing like getting a man with the dogs. Mine aren't bloodhounds, though the ignorant call them that. They're part mastiff and Great Pyrenees and part staghound. You remember that little escapee about two years ago? Why, Marshall, they had him half eaten before we got to him. They tore four-and six-pound hunks of meat right out of him. They tore out hunks of meat with bones in it. A man is mighty loud when you do that to him. You can have any other sort of poetry. A coon doesn't scream like that when you kill him. A badger doesn't. Even a big cat doesn't. A man-kill is best—for the very noise he makes. I like a man to scream that way.''

"This one won't scream that way, Crocker. I don't think so. He's a bear or a bugger or a monster, but not a man. We may, however, hear a howling and roaring such as hasn't been heard on Earth since the primordial days. He says that they've been here before. You hunt your way and I'll hunt mine, and we'll see who latches onto him first. But remember. I get to finish him.''

They hadn't just been talking. They had been bisecting the country again and again, going on the dirt and gravel section lines, taking the huge hounds out of the panel-car at favorable points to try to cut the Dulanty trail. They'd have that mad killer. They'd be onto him any minute.

And they had a dozen other crews out looking for Henry Dulanty; and there were roadblocks on everything from a lane to a deer trail.

Henry Dulanty came to himself in a dark wood where the straight way was lost. He either heard or imagined that he heard the distant sounding of hounds. There is an ancient antipathy between Pucas and every sort of dogs, but especially the great hounds. Henry would have welcomed the conflict with a pack of them, were they not to be backed up by men with guns. He could smash them as well as the biggest bear could. He'd be well-blooded in doing it, of course, but he believed that that was just what he needed. A bloody life battle might cleanse his humors from the Earth Sickness and make him a full Puca again.

Henry was content to remain lost. He believed that there was no one near him, and that he could shamble along till full strength and intelligence might return to him for a while.

Then, in a glimmer of starlight, he saw a man or a demiurge growing out of the ground. It winked at him. It seemed a deeper thing than the regular people, but it was not a Puca.

"It would be easier to use the path," the apparition said. "You've been going through some pretty hard brush and making a hellish noise."

"I imagined I was moving in perfect silence." Henry said, "but my powers are at low ebb. I'd use a path if I could find one, and if it were going where I wanted to go—something I'm not sure of. And if they don't have roadblocks on it yet."

"It's too slight a path for them to know to block," the creature said. (It was as big as Henry, and rough-hewn.)

141

"There is only one place to go. I'll go with you and show you the way. We'd better start along. It's less than three hours till they close."

"Whatever are the gates that close in three hours, they might not be those I intend to enter," Henry said. But he was going with the man. (It was a man after all. He may have had a little bark on him, but he was not actually growing out of the ground.)

"What is Crocker out hunting?" the rough-hewn man asked as they followed the slight path. "He usually doesn't come this far from his base."

"He's hunting me," Henry said. "Can you hear the hounds? I wasn't sure that I could, and I've been listening."

"I can't hear them yet, and neither can you. I can smell them, though. A creature that can't smell them farther than he can hear them deserves to be taken."

"He doesn't deserve to be taken on all counts," Henry said. "What are you called?"

"John Lewis Grew," said the preternatural creature.

"I thought I knew all the dimiurges, Greek, Roman, Hindu, and primordial, but I don't place your name among them."

"I'm a Quapaw. They all call me John Loose Screw after the sound of my name. I don't like it, but I can't stop it. You'll be doing it, too, after five minutes. I tell you though, I have no more loose screws than the rest of them have."

They walked. It was brighter now and the trees thinned out. The man was wearing a shaggy jacket and he had a certain roughness in his finish, but it wasn't bark growing on him.

"What closes in three hours?" Henry asked as they came to a dimly neoned shanty. "I wouldn't walk into a

142

trap, but I need a shelter.''

"The Lost Moon Bar, of course," said John Loose Screw. "It has to close at one o'clock. We're going to have to drink pretty fast. We have less than three hours."

It seemed to be a very local place, and it might be safe for a while. They went in. It was a small barroom full of big Indians. John Loose Screw made a sign to the man behind the bar, and that man began to draw forth and fill various types of glasses.

These were Henry's kind of people. He knew them in the brazenness of the tactic. It isn't pulled on just anybody, only on the visiting Chieftain thus challenged to stand and produce. Henry admired the ease and assurance of its execution.

It was the tactic of the Presumptive Assumption which has its roots midway between the Pragmatic Sanction and the Categorical Imperative. They knew Henry instantly, and he knew them.

"I have counted the house," John Loose Screw told Henry when the thing was already in motion in the little crossroads Indian tavern. "For four dollars and thirty cents you can set them up. I would do it if I had four dollars and thirty cents."

So Henry Dulanty set up beer and drinks for the timeless Indians in the Lost Moon Bar, and so doing he stored up merit for himself in Heaven.

"Where have you guys been?" the man behind the bar asked Henry.

"You mean John Loose Screw and myself?"

"No. I mean you and your people," the barman said. "We waited for you and you didn't come. Quite a while back, one of you said that a bunch of you would be along, and you'd help us set up a system. But you didn't show."

"No. Our home camp was raided several times and our

143

plans partly lost,'' Henry said. ''Then, when we were ready to undertake things again, our information was jumbled. I'm not the sort of being who should have been sent to this country in this century. I should have been sent to a place where the people still live a little nearer the ground.''

''Up to a thousand years ago we could have made this half of the apple a pretty good place,'' the barman said. ''We could have held it for our own increase and built it up in all proper time. Up to a hundred and fifty years ago we might still have pulled it off—jack-jumped the White Eyes and chased them into the sea. But even then it would have been pretty tricky and would have left hard feelings. Now it's too late.''

''I didn't realize you'd recognize me,'' Henry said.

''Oh, you're in the Grandmother Stories of most of the tribes.''

Well, they were a reserved but friendly bunch here. You had *better* have those men for your friends, or stay out of their den. Henry saw that he might not be able to master things here in a showdown; he wouldn't have been able to do it even if he had been well. Henry could take a dozen men of a certain sort even now. But John Loose Screw, the man behind the bar, and a long young man in a sports coat were men of another sort. They were horned-bull men all!

And the rest of the men there were the biggest, most bulging, sly-grinning, sleepy-eyed men he had ever seen in one room at one time. It would have been like coming against one dozen Mandrake Marshalls, and without the moment of full strength that was granted to Henry when he tangled with Marshall that time.

''I won't be able to stay very long, John Loose Screw,'' Henry said, raising his head and apprehending. ''They'll close me up long before one o'clock. In just three minutes there will be a great baying, and a meute of hounds and mastiffs will be onto my trail here. They will be baying for me. I can't hear them or smell them, but I have my own sensing.''

"How do you know then?'' the long young man in the sports coat asked. "What kind of crystal ball do you have?''

"A sixteen-inch one, friend, half meter trade size,'' Henry answered, "Venetian depth glass, panoramic viewer, futuristic correlator, cosmic filter, not real fancy.''

"What's the cosmic filter for?'' the young man asked.

"It gets rid of all that side talk from outer space.''

"You're kidding,'' the young man said seriously. "But are you the one? Are they coming with the dogs for you?''

"Yes. Pretty quickly now. I know how Crocker trains them. They're pretty savage. So is he and whoever will be with him. They have my scent now. I hear them going crazy where they cut my trail. I need a break.''

"I'd just as soon become involved,'' that long young man said. "I like to get involved in things. You're the Mad Killer, are you? There's some pretty good rewards out for you, and they get bigger as the night goes on. Crocker and Marshall have each offered a thousand dollars for you. Of course neither of them would pay, but they've posted it.

"But Joe Coon behind the bar there wouldn't like it if anybody here took money for a man. John Loose Screw wouldn't like it. I wouldn't like it either. If the three of us don't like a thing, nobody here's going to do it. I see an ear twitch here and there, but they're not going to inform.

"I've seen you before. I watched your kids one day and talked to them. It was a circus. I don't know what kind of things you are, but I like you better than the White Eyes around this country. Let's go."

That young man was big, and he moved like a lion to the door.

"All right," Henry said, "but where?"

"I got a car outside that will do a hundred and thirty-nine miles an hour, real speed," the young man said. "The speedometer's the only thing in it not set fast. I can go through any roadblock they set up. I got a chrome-plated dozer blade on the front of my bus, and a vertical slicer. It's the sportiest-looking front in the world, and it'll kindle any block. It can run away and leave the world standing still."

(There is belief that the Indians had fast cars before the Flood. They remembered them more than did other people when mankind was reconstituted, and more than other people they know what to do with them.)

"—and look what it will do from a standing start!" the young man cried ten seconds later. Henry was now in the fast car with the sports-coated young man. "I have thrown gravel a measured two hundred feet on takeoff," the young man continued, "and I have burned rubber for ninety-seven feet on the pavement. This car is steel-looped and cross-looped. It can roll over and come up still running wide open. It has armored body, shot-proof glass, self-sealing tires, astatic cigarette trays, flame-retarding neoprene-sealed gas tank, auxiliary boosters, all-bands radio, and a telephone—with unlisted number."

"Have you considered a gyroscopic stabilizer to put it on automatic pilot if you black out? Or a bank-angle analyzer to permit it to take turns on automatic?" Henry asked, very much interested.

"Considered it? Man, I've got it," the young man said. "Built everything myself. I'm a mechanical engineer, Oklahoma State '63. It's got a photoelectric control to make it swerve to miss cows and hogs in the road when it's on automatic, and it embodies a prediction factor to detect which way a hog will break. That's important when you're driving on automatic at night."

They went through a roadblock at high speed. The young man had been right. That chrome slicer on front would kindle any block. They were shot at from both front and back with some high-powered stuff. It did have shot-proof glass, and not only to turn little pop-pistol shot as the dealers will show you sometimes. It did have a self-sealing gas tank with flame-retarding neoprene sheath. It had better have!

It was an interesting but rather rough ride, and they talked of other devices that would really jazz up a car. But when they came to a stop, the trouble wasn't the car wouldn't do a full roll easily, it was that it would do a roll and a half easier. The car slid a hundred and ninety feet on its top before it came to a stop against an embankment. It was a well-built car, but it wouldn't be running any more that night.

The young man told Henry to go ahead and leave him; that all he had was a broken collarbone; that he broke it every time he turned the car over; that he was, in fact, collarbone-broke prone.

And the blood on him was nothing, he insisted. He always got a lot of blood on him.

"But it was an interesting talk," the young man said. "I love to talk to anybody who is mechanically inclined. I'm going to put in an automatic pressurizer and a standby oxygen supply in case I ever end up upside down in the bottom of a lake. I'm going to put a scanner-pilot on it also. Just put a checkmark on a road-map where you want to go, and feed the map into its gullet. It'll take you there by the most direct route, and even pick the roadside stops with the best meals. If they don't kill you tonight, come around again. I'd like to know you better.

"Say, you'd better take off! They'll have us picked up with headlights in a matter of seconds. Oh Hell yes, I'm all right. This happens to me all the time."

So Henry Dulanty crawled out of the upside-down car and was on his way again, more lost than ever.

The young man's name is Sammy Bluefield. You might meet him sometime, and then you'll know who he is.

14

Fit Subject for Heroic Chantey

So Big Henry Dulanty was in the woods again, but a dozen miles away from the other woods. It might be some time before they got hounds on his new trail. But someone would know what region he was in. Sammy Bluefield might flub the men with the story that he had been alone in the car—that he had been off on a frolic of his own. But Henry was certain that the men at the crashed roadblock had lighted them up good enough with their spotlights to see that there had been two men in the car.

Every car would be stopped on every road. And every road down to the meanest section line was being picked out with headlights. Every bridge and almost every culvert was manned. It is hard to travel any distance without crossing either over or under some road. In theory, Henry Dulanty would be boxed into one of the gridded sections of land, and could be tracked down there as soon as the dogs could cut his trail again.

But that country was not as even as the theory might indicate. Much of it was hilly, the roads following the contours of the land and not the straight section lines; and headlights, picking out the roads, could reach no further than the crest of the next hill. It was a strategy game between Henry Dulanty and quite a few hunting men, played out for the Dulanty life.

But all the men of the country were not out on the hunt. The majority cowered in their homes in town and country and listened to radios or TV while the Mad Killer stalked their region.

There was quite a bit of terror that night in the rolling bluestem country; and the dogs caught the fright from their masters, and whined and carried on.

The dogs, but not the Dogs yet.

There are some dogs that pay no attention to the Puca at all, indeed seem not to see them or sense them in any way. Many dogs hate the Puca. Others go crazy with fear of them. Henry had to be careful in his choice of a farm and dog. He wanted a reasonable man who would agree to hide him for several days until the vigilance relaxed.

Henry sampled half a dozen farmsteads and left them alone. He had, under the window of one of them, heard the broadcast of his own activities as the Mad Killer. There were stony and unseeing dogs, there were furious dogs, there were terrified dogs, guarding the various farmsteads. Then he came to a farmhouse that had a finely bred, strongly built, slightly stupid dog who barked only a little and stood on bristling formality.

"The man will be of the same sort," Henry told himself, "middling good, hard to scare, and a little stupid. No dog ever differs much from his master, and no bad dog ever had a good master. I'll go in and take my chances if the man is at home. If he isn't home, I'll take my chances anyhow."

The house was dark. There was no answer to the low hallow, so Henry attempted the place. The front door was unlocked. Henry opened it noiselessly—knowing at once, however, that someone was standing and watching him from the darkness. "Good evening," Henry said in the direction of the invisible man.

Then Henry was hit in the face by a ball of light.

"Raise your hands very high," said the man of the house. He had a five-cell flashlight in one hand and a .45 in the other. With what must have been a third hand, or perhaps an elbow, he flicked on the main lights of the room.

It was a good-sized man of full middle-age, probably scared—as believing the Mad Killer bit—but steady.

"Stand over there against the wall with your back to me," the man said to Henry.

On the Sands of Hesitation—

Henry still had his Puca speed. He could have struck before the man could have reacted with his gun. He could have made the man a prisoner and stayed on there awkwardly. Or he could bind or disable the man and leave, and try his luck somewhere else. He could go on felling men all night, and keep moving till he was caught.

But he wanted to negotiate a refuge. He wanted a man to hide him in an inner upper room where his scent might be masked, a man who would lie for him and swear to all comers that the Mad Killer had indeed come to the door, but had then talked incoherently, and had gone back the way he had come.

Henry could quickly instruct the man in little things, how his scent over the threshold and inside the house might be disguised by wheat bran or shorts sprinkled lightly and swept up again, or by a dozen things to be found around any Earther house.

Henry Dulanty, as he should have been, could have dominated almost any man with words. But the Earthsick Henry had become almost fumbling in his speech and thoughts. He would have to gamble time and wait for the next temporary return of his powers. He stood over there against the wall with his back to the man.

"Do not try anything," the man said nervously.

"I will try anything, even reason," Henry answered.

"Are you Henry Dulanty?"

"I am a stranger lost."

"I am placing you under citizen's arrest."

"Let me see proof of your citizenship."

"You're Henry Dulanty all right. It's been said that you're an incurable scoffer."

"And the Mad Killer at the same time?"

"That's right. A scoffing sort of cunning might go with madness."

The man patted Henry over his pockets and under his armpits and on the inside of his legs and all such places.

On the Sands of Hesitation—

"What did you do with it?" the man asked.

"Explicitness is a forgotten virtue," Henry said.

"There you go smarting off again. What did you do with the gun you took off the jailer?"

Broached and Breached the Craft Dulanty—

"I took no gun," Henry said.

"The alert says that you took it," the man insisted, "and that you are a Mad Man, armed and dangerous." He was a fair-sized man, fifty years and a day old, a leading citizen you would say at once, and a fool.

Panged by Pygmies, Irked by Earthman—

"If you believe that I took the gun, then you're dead already," Henry said. "The two things tie together."

"Do not threaten me," said the man. "Take off your pants and shirt! Do it now!"

He the Monster, by the Midgets—

"To be closeted with a fool!" Henry muttered, but he did as he was told. He took off his pants and shirt. The man was not green. He could use the gun.

152

On a Farmstead Near Catoosa—

"Toss them across the room here," the man ordered, "and make no false move." Henry tossed the stuff over. The man went through it carefully, and then examined the shaggy-bare Henry Dulanty. "That's peculiar," the man said. "You didn't have a gun after all. What did you do with it?"

In a Trap, Who'd Ambled Planets—

"If you believe that I had a gun, then you believe it to your death," Henry said sadly.

"Don't give me riddles, Dulanty. Lie down on the floor with your head in the corner while I phone the authorities to come for you."

Finding Time Beshorn of Forelock—

Henry Dulanty, wondering at himself in his sickness, lay down on the floor. He would have to convince this fool.

"Tell them one thing, for your own sake," Henry said carefully. "To send the sheriff, and nobody else, or only those of his group. Tell them to contact the sheriff by phone and not over the air. Marshall and Crocker are likely to pick up anything that goes to the sheriff over the air. Have them notify the sheriff only, if you have the telephone disease. On no account have them notify Crocker or Marshall."

De Profundis in Patinam—

"Shut up, Dulanty. They will send who they will send." The man was on the phone. He talked to somebody, and was satisfied. "Everybody knows where my place is," he kept saying. "It's been called the Butterfield place for a hundred years. Get somebody here quick." He was satisfied when he hung up. "Somebody will be here pretty quick," he said to the room and to Henry Dulanty, "whichever of them is driving nearest when they get the

153

information by radio.''

Stewed in Stifling Introspection–

''Have you a name?'' Henry Dulanty asked the man.

''Thomas Butterfield. It's an old name here.''

''Thomas, let me explain. If you let me go, or hide me and say that I have gone, you can save your own life. If you do not let me go, you cannot save your own life, not if Marshall gets here first.''

Stream of Thought–the Earthen Sickness–

''How is my life in any danger, Dulanty? It isn't from you.''

''I haven't the time to be impatient with you, Butterfield. If it was announced that I took the gun from the jailer, then it was announced for a reason. It was Marshall himself giving the broadcasts when I listened. Likely Marshall took the gun himself from the jailer to plant it on me. If he is the one who comes for he, he'll kill me here. He's eaten up with lust for it.''

Lost the Swiftness of the Puca–

''You will see him do it, Thomas,'' Henry continued, ''and you will know that I was unarmed and that it was unnecessary to kill me. He can't leave you alive to give testimony against him. He will stage it neatly to make it seem that I killed you with the jailer's gun, which he will plant in my hand when it is still warm.''

Stranded Like a Fool, Dulanty–

''I know Marshall quite well,'' Butterfield said. ''He's a fine man, and your whole story is a ridiculous fabrication.''

''Does it irritate you, Butterfield, when somebody tells you how a story or a play will end?''

On the Reefs of Earth–Untimely–

''It does. Why?''

''I have just told you how your story will end. Well,

enough of that, Butterfield. I have to leave you in a hurry now. It may already be too late."

Henry Dulanty rose from the floor and began to put on his clothes.

"Dulanty, I tell you I'll kill you right now," Butterfield said. "I'm not afraid."

"I am, a little bit, but not of you."

"Dulanty, I swear to God, you leave me no choice!"

Passed the Final Fatal Moment—

"Don't intend to. If you're going to shoot, do it now. I'm in a hurry."

"Dulanty, you drive me to it!"

But Thomas Butterfield, like Henry Dulanty himself, had waited too long. And he didn't know how fast Henry Dulanty could move. Henry slapped the .45 out of his hand and then felled him with a stunning blow.

"I've got a chance," Henry said. "It's coming back to me. I'm going to have another moment of strength. In just an instant I'll know what to do again.

"No—my chance just melted. I know his footsteps in the yard. I hadn't even heard the dogs, I was so listless. He's a fool for luck. He must have been driving very near when he got the call. It comes back to me, but not fast enough."

Henry started for the .45 which had slid under a sofa, and at the same time he started for a little door to gain the interior of the house. It was his last indecision, for Mandrake Marshall was already in the room.

Piger Tempus Edax Rerum—

Henry Dulanty pitched forward onto his face when the first of Marshall's shots caught him high in the shoulder from behind. That laughing man Marshall fairly bristled with the bloodlust in him.

"Get up, Dulanty!" Marshall barked, like one of the

chorus of hounds still held leashed by Crocker. "A shot like that doesn't hurt a man like you! You're got a dozen more coming."

"You shouldn't have shot him in the back, Marshall," Crocker panted, still holding the dogs. "Shots in the back are always hard to explain as self-defense."

"Shut up, Crocker! Hello, Butterfield. If that's not the suit you want to die in, you have time to go change. You do want to look nice, don't you? Come get me, Dulanty! You old animal, let's see how you charge."

Door of Time Against the Puca—

Henry Dulanty came up on his feet. His Puca strength had returned, but only in time for him to die in it. He charged dumbly and in pain, and went down from a groin shot by Marshall. Marshall shot very fast. Crocker had tied the dogs to a porch pillar, and now held a rifle in readiness.

"Marshall," said Thomas Butterfield, coming out of his daze. "That man is not armed. You can confine him without shooting."

"Shut up, Butterfield. Those your death duds, are they? Come on, Dulanty! You disappoint me. Up we come! Onto your feet once more! Here I am! Come get me!"

Ensorceled Earth—a Bomb Inside You—

Henry Dulanty was on his feet again, and then down once more, gut-shot by Marshall.

"Too many shots are hard to explain," Crocker said dryly. "You're excited, Marshall. Finish him off this time, and then change guns for Butterfield here."

"In my own way, Crocker," Marshall panted. "Come on Dulanty! One more time! Come get a piece of me—you think!"

Dragons' Children Hatching, Growing—

Henry was up again, but wobbly. He knew that he was dying, but he had a sudden humor to spook his killer in dying. He moved three steps almost too fast to follow, then stumbled and grappled into Marshall, falling, and sending a sudden wave of fear through that man. Marshall screamed, but Crocker shot Dulanty in the face. Crocker was cool as ice when there was killing to be done. Henry Dulanty fell and lay still.

"What's a goblin like inside, Dulanty?" Marshall shouted, quickly recovering from one insanity into another.

"Let's spill you out a little more and see."

"That's enough," said Crocker. "He's dead. Don't mark him up any more. This much will be hard enough to explain."

Come the Green-Eyes, Come Requiting—

Henry's shot face had become somewhat unhuman in repose, but not less than human. The Dulantys could manage to look like regular people, till they had to laugh, or die.

"That's enough, Marshall," Crocker repeated. "The dogs have been done out of their due. I'd as soon put them on you as him. Take Butterfield now."

Nil de Monstris Nisi Bonum.

Thomas Butterfield was sickened by the way Marshall had killed Henry Dulanty, but he still couldn't understand that it would turn out fatally for himself. He wondered how Marshall would explain the killing of an unarmed man to the world, but he simply gazed.

Then Marshall changed guns. He held the jailer's handgun now. When the realization came to Butterfield, it was like ice.

"You can't kill me," he said seriously. "I voted for you once."

Mandrake Marshall laughed and shot. It was the predictable end of the Butterfield story.

One. And two. Marshall had had a good night. He looked at Crocker. Should he try for three?

15

The Battle Joined That Could But Leave

Crocker was delirious. He couldn't sleep after he had been dropped off at his place by Marshall, and his dogs couldn't sleep. There was something worrying and unsatisfied in them all. Crocker was still apprehensive about what the lawyer from T-Town and Frank Dulanty and the drunk Fronsac had turned up.

Marshall hadn't followed through the previous night as to taking care of Frank Dulanty. The broadcasts on the Mad Brother of the Mad Killer had died out when Marshall became temporarily sated of the killing.

But there wasn't any very good way that Crocker and Frank Dulanty could both keep living in the world. One of them plainly would have to die. But Crocker, between the noose of Frank and the legal threat of murder trial, still wasn't whipped.

Those several men who had almost been persuaded to give evidence against Crocker yesterday could never be persuaded again. Henry Dulanty, who had been given to the popular mind as the killer of Thomas Butterfield, must also be left undisturbed in that mind as the killer of Coalfactor Stutgard. The neatness of tying everything to Henry Dulanty the Mad Killer could hardly be challenged, now that he was dead.

But there was always the worry over Mandrake Marshall. This was another of those mutually exclusive deals: either Marshall or Crocker had to die, and they both knew it. There could not be a double inheritance to the realm of Coalfactor Stutgard. And this ultimatum worried Crocker more than it did Marshall.

Crocker was also in terror of three Dulantys. Had not Henry, after his face was broken and he looked at them through a red glaze, said, 'You haven't seen the last of me, I'll be back,' or had Crocker only imagined it? Crocker was usually cool during a killing, but the aftermath produced illusions of things both present and past. In the dying face of Henry Dulanty, turning unhuman as he died, there had been the impression of great powers that could perhaps transcend these barriers.

And there was still Frank Dulanty in his first threat—that of the noose he had put around Crocker's neck. The noose remained there invisible. And Crocker still had the noose itself on his bedpost, and it stared at him.

And there was the small Dulanty boy who had looked in at him in Stutgard's upstairs room. It is disquieting to look up from the business of murder and find yourself observed. But it hadn't been that which made his hair absolutely stand on end and which still haunted him now.

Crocker hadn't simply seen the little boy; he had seen through him at the same time. In his delirium Crocker saw it all again. That little boy had been standing on air, and he had been transparent. He was not made out of flesh. He was made out of whatever deliriums are made of.

A bedlam of such things paced up and down in Crocker's head, while his hounds also paced and grumbled at being done out of their part of the murders. So Crocker hit the old panther, and got what sleep he could out of it.

● ● ●

In the morning, Crocker rose very early and drunkenly. He dressed, though awkwardly and with mismatched boots. He gathered his seven dogs, took along a rifle and the noose and a bottle of the old cat-creature, and went out to find and kill the transparent little boy so he could sleep nights.

Crocker knew generally where those Dulanty kids were hiding out. At least he knew what sector his impressors had not returned from. And he had clothing of the smallest of the Dulanty boys that he had taken from the Big Shanty on the night of the attempted lynching of Frank Dulanty. His hounds were worrying the rags, and knew who they were to find.

"There is a man sitting on top of Misu Mound," Dorothy said. "He has branches growing out of the top of his head. I never saw anything like that before."

"Oh, it's Fulbert," Helen explained. "He comes there lots of days, and I'm always the only one alert enough to notice it. He never had branches growing out of the top of his head before, though. It's something to think about. Do you suppose that's what alcoholism does in its last stages, Peter?"

"No. He's wearing them for camouflage. He's acting as lookout for us. Maybe he doesn't understand that we already have one of those old dead Indians acting as lookout."

"Maybe he'll get so drunk that he'll roll down off the mountain and into the river," said John. "Then we'll vote on whether to hold him under water and drown him or drag him out and save him. I vote we drown him."

"No. He's used to being that way," Peter said. "You never see an experienced drunk fall off a mountain. You can hear Crocker's dogs now. He's out hunting us early."

161

●●●

The three mastiffs of Crocker were named Bell, Book, and Candle. The four hounds, smaller than the mastiffs but still large, were Luke, John, Barnabas, and Timothy. What had happened to the earlier Matthew and Mark is two other bloody stories (one of an old boar coon, one of a young fast bear); but the younger dogs, Barnabas and Timothy, were good ones.

The dogs had the scent of that smallest boy again, but it led into boggy ground that would not support even the lightest of the dogs.

"He is quite a small boy," Crocker said, "but not that small. He cannot be weightless. If a hound would go down here, a boy would go down here too. Well, they've picked up his spoor on the other side of the morass now, but then it heads into even softer places."

Crocker, though he didn't know there were two of them, was tracking Bad John and not John. He was after his proper prey, but he didn't understand its nature. So he worked that morning with his dogs on the trail of the small boy he had to kill.

Now and then, after Crocker and his hounds had circled onto firm ground and once more picked up the trail beyond, the eight hunters would sit down to rest. Then Crocker would console himself with Spirits of Panther (called Horse Whisky by the vulgar); and sometimes he slept.

Once, when he had slept for a minute and wakened with a start, he saw the small boy standing and watching him not thirty yards away. There was something at once wretched and appealing and defiant about that little Dulanty boy. Crocker fired quickly, and the boy disappeared. He didn't fall; he thinned out to nothingness.

"I'm coming apart," Crocker said. "I'm firing at

ghosts. But I see everything else clear, and I saw him transparent.''

But still he pushed on with his seven restive dogs, circling deeper and deeper into the bogs after a prey who followed a rambling and impossible course.

''Old Crocker is lost,'' Fronsac said as he watched from the top of Misu Mound. ''In another hour or two he'll be in where he can never get out. Then I'll go down and claim one of the dogs.''

''Is Candle the one you want?'' the old dead Indian asked.

''Yes, Candle. I never saw such an animal. He blazes at night.''

''I'd like to own him myself, if I were not beyond the state of owning,'' the old Indian said. ''Crocker hunts his prey which he cannot come up to. But another hunts Crocker. You know?''

''I know.''

''And another follows the man who follows Crocker. And a fourth hunter waits in ambush for the third. You believe you have it figured out, but you have missed one of the persons entirely. I wonder if you would pour me a little of that, Fronsac, no more than an acorn-full. I no longer have the equipment to handle it, but I love the taste. Ah, White Lightning, that splits the skull and encourages the body and the sentiments!''

''It is my pleasure,'' said Fronsac. ''I never liked to drink alone. My little urchins on the rafts will drift away tonight, and Witchy may be with them. Do you think the world is safe from them?''

''I don't know, Fronsac. I wouldn't care if they roughed up the old orb a little. They're an intriguing bunch. That Helen had an argument with one of our ladies

163

(and damned if it doesn't seem that she used to be one of my wives) about a thighbone. 'It's just barely fastened on,' Helen insisted, 'you're allowed to take them if they're just barely fastened on.' 'No, no,' my old wife howled, 'it's part of me. I've lost so many bones that I want to keep that one. Go away, little girl.' 'But I want to make an artifact out of it,' Helen said, 'it's just the right size. Here, I'll give you a buffalo thighbone in place of it.' She did, and I tell you that my old wife hobbles around pretty grotesquely now with that buffalo thighbone, and everybody laughs at her. We laugh at things like that now. We haven't much else.''

There are those who say that Fulbert couldn't talk to the old dead Indians in Misu Mound at all; that he was a degenerate drunk who went up on the mountain and talked to himself and had fantasies because he was a rummy.

But if you're going to call everybody a rummy who talks to dead Indians you're going to defame a lot of very good people.

After a while, Fulbert made a signal that only one of the six Dulantys saw and interpreted. And Charles Dulanty slipped off from the rest of them to play his hand.

Puca dramas differ in pace and climax from the dramas of Earth people. In the high classic form, there is always a scene (very near the end) where all the bloody stuff is heaped together for the greater enjoyment and convenience of all. It is extravagant and outré. It is both tragic and comic in the tall burlesque of it. It thrills the liver and entrails and heart of the Pucas. And to Earth people it would seem rather crude and excessive.

Be you not offended! Through a miracle of circumstance, we now live for short moments through the outré scene of a classic Puca drama. A suddenly hooded sun gave a garish light for the scene. It is always so.

The next time that Crocker sat down to rest and sleep, he was unaccountably chilly. He was on a bank above the worst of the bogs, one impossible either to cross or to circuit. Yet here the scent of the small boy led straight ahead. He was under an old sycamore tree that had lost most of its hide and showed only stark white branches.

He slept once and met Stutgard; he forced himself awake barely in time to escape him. That man would have killed him in his sleep.

One of the hounds, Barnabas, trailed away and left Crocker for good. Dogs will abandon a disintegrating man so.

When Crocker slept again he met Marshall, lusting for a Crocker-kill. Crocker walked in panic to avoid him. Each time it became more difficult to wake up, and more necessary to do so. Death might attend the sleeping for only an extra second. The other three hounds trailed off, and only the mastiffs were left. Crocker noticed for the first time that his boots were not matched.

''Here I am, either two different men, or I have one foot each of two different men,'' he said. ''I knew I was coming apart, but I didn't imagine it would be like this.''

In his next sleep, Crocker saw the small boy who floated over the bogs. He woke with extreme effort, and was soaked in clammy sweat. But when awake he still saw the boy. This caused him to doubt whether he was asleep or awake, and this doubt remained with him for the short scrap of his life that was left.

Crocker slept again and dreamed of Frank Dulanty. He was even colder than he had been before. Then an unseen hand came and wrapped a scarf around his neck.

''Thank you for your unintended kindness,'' Crocker

said. "There is more here than meets the eye or touches the neck, but I cannot fathom it. I'd have frozen to death without it."

It fit snugly and smelled hempen and had not the feel of an ordinary scarf. Crocker wakened into a shallower sleep and knew that it was Frank Dulanty behind him. It was the noose around his neck, and no scarf. The line of it went over one of the bone-white branches of the sycamore.

"What do you intend to do, Dulanty?" Crocker asked rationally without looking around.

"Kill you, and then find the children," Frank said as evenly. "They'll have received the blood message by now, and may have some thought of revenge. I must instruct them to deal gently with the world. During my tour of Earth, I have decided that perhaps we ourselves are a little ruthless. I'll advise them to look for a broader way than I have found. Now rouse yourself, Crocker, and walk down into the bog. I'll leave you just enough slack for it."

Book and Bell trailed off, and only Candle was left.

"This is murder," Crocker said, "ironic as it seems, coming from me."

"No. Into the bog, I say, Crocker. The court that was to sit today did not sit, and I have supplied its lack. The men who will be afraid to testify in open court have already testified privately to me. You killed Stutgard and, more important, you killed my brother."

"No, not him. Marshall killed Henry. I only watched."

"Marshall? I've missed part of this. It seemed too direct and massive a thing for you to pull. How does Marshall come to be killing people he hardly knows? It worries me that I may have underestimated him in other ways. So, my work is only half done when I kill you."

Crocker was up to his loins in the gob. His arms

166

trembled, and his hands slipped on the rope.

"There's one thing you've overlooked, Dulanty," he said thickly. "I can wake up and make you go away."

"It's worth a try, Crocker. Go ahead."

But Crocker couldn't. Frank tightened the rope for the last time, and Crocker pulled himself up a little from the bog on very weary arms.

A lion can move more quietly than a jackal, especially one who has just graduated into the role of local lion. He can move more quietly than a hound, and soundless to an intent man. Mandrake Marshall, the man underestimated by Frank Dulanty, chewed on a stem of weed and looked thoughtful.

"The show drags a little," he said to himself. "We'd better run the curtain down before the audience becomes restive. I am the audience."

Then his calmness exploded, and he became a madman at the new opportunity.

Marshall hit Frank Dulanty a terrific blow on the back of the head with his rifle butt. The blow was one of the really colossal things. He may have killed Frank with the one blow.

"I never felt strong against you as I did your brother," Marshall said as he looked down at Frank, calm and satisfied again. That man turned madness on and off like a tap. "It never seemed like you had as much of the beast in you. Ah, but you're one of them too. You get the look more when you're dead. You're a loose end, Frank. I couldn't leave you lying around."

The line had slipped from Frank's hand and whipped like a snake over the sycamore limb. Every foot of it was gobbled up by the fast-disappearing Crocker. Marshall made no move to save his partner in crime, and Crocker went down wide-eyed and frozen.

"You should have screamed, you devil," Marshall complained to the disappeared Crocker. You cheated me there.

"We'll just roll you down this bank, Dulanty," Marshall continued. "I liked to roll down banks when I was a little boy. Things like this bring out the boy in me."

He rolled Frank down the bank and into the bog, pushing him out a ways into it as he sank.

"Hello, Candle," Marshall greeted the last dog. "You're a good animal and I meant to have you a long time ago. You belong to me now. I'd like to have the boy too, but I'm not sure I can swing that one. We'll see."

The boy was shooting at Marshall from a distance and running as he shot.

"The first thing I'd teach him would be not to fire blindly while running across the country like that, not to fire without aiming, and not to fire before coming into range," Marshall lectured himself. "He's the son of one of them. Hey, the species does stand out on them when they're angry! I doubt if I could own him like a dog, but it'd be fun to kill the father and then take his pup. Like to raise that Puca my way. They've a lot of juice in them. Admit it, Mandrake, you were jealous that they had more animal in them than you did.

"He should have two shots left, and he's going to save them till he's in range. He's no fool."

Charles Dulanty had learned, possibly in the direct way that Puca learn things, possibly from Fulbert Fronsac, that Crocker would be out hunting the wraith child Bad John (whom he could never catch); that Frank Dulanty would be hunting Crocker (but slowly, as to allow him to come to his physical breakup first); and that another man would be trailing Frank. Fulbert and Charles had set up the signal

168

together, and Fulbert from his lookout was to warn when Frank's hunter appeared.

What neither of them knew was how fast Marshall moved. He came at a pace that was neither a stride nor a trot, topping crest after crest with silent speed, killing Frank before either warning could be raised or counterattack launched. Charles had seen the end of Crocker and of Frank. Now he was running in a fury, but he thought coolly at the same time. He'd kill Marshall with a little luck. It was his to do. He had become, at eight years old, the patriach of the Dulanty clan. It would never have occurred to his cousin Peter to challenge him. The leader moves naturally into leadership when the time comes.

"He's serious," Marshall said, half reading the thoughts of the running boy. "And he knows what he's doing. He's a hard target running through the reeds; but when he takes the next crest I'll have him. The rifle's too heavy for him. He's betting he can hit the ground in time when I level. It'd be a good bet with any man but me. He doesn't know how fast I can level."

Charles had half taken the crest. Watch! It's fast—like three snakes striking at once! Marshall leveled, aimed, and fired with one motion. It was a curious blast—like three instantaneous shots in one. Check the bodies. See who's down.

Charles had used his next to last shot just before he hit the ground. It rang in his ears much louder than it should have—with an authority that had no counterpart in the recoil. It didn't feel like a good shot. But Marshall had jerked upward curiously in the act of firing; and now he was down. And he was dead.

Charles came forward cautiously, shaking his head and scattering leaves and fronds. He had at first believed that Marshall's shot had scotched him in the head; but it had only split fragments from a small boulder and then rattled into a small tree, showering Charles with various light debris.

"I'm a better shot than I thought," Charles said as he sidled up and examined the last dead man. "A lot better. It seemed like I hit him an instant before I pulled the trigger. And the funniest thing about it is that he was hit by a thirty long, from the way it tore into him, and I was shooting shorts."

Charles examined the body with great curiosity, having never seen a dead adult of the Earth species before.

"Say, that tore into his head and mighty near exploded there, and came out ten times as big as it went in. I wonder if brains are really good for catfish bait, or was Helen just jiving those boys the other day? If I had a scoop I'd scoop it full of them."

Charles made a pry from an old branch and rolled Marshall over and over down the bank and into the bog. And he watched the big man sink.

"It's going to be getting a little bit crowded in that bog," Charles said, "and there aren't any of them very friendly to each other."

At the same time, and not thirty yards away, Phoebe Jane Lanyard ejected a shell from her rifle. She was smiling a quivering smile that turned inward at the corners, and then inward again. Did you know that Indians have an expression very like Pucas when they have just killed someone? It's near the same look.

She wasn't free from bloodlust herself. She'd never liked Marshall at all.

"Now I'll go home and get out the old car and go up to Vinita," she said to herself, "and shuck Witchy over the wall of that booby-hatch after dark, and bring her to join the children. Then they'll be gone."

• • •

The afternoon sun came out clear again. The *aerach*, the outer scene of the classic Puca drama, was over with.

16

Or Altered World or Dead Dulanty

"We will cast off at moonrise, or at another rising a few seconds later," Charles announced late that afternoon. "See to all the battenings and lashings. It will be a long voyage. Phoebe Jane says she will bring us some other things in a boat just after dark. You, first and second mate (that was Elizabeth and Peter, but Helen was navigator), please make a detailed inspection and report to me on the bridge if anything is amiss."

Charles was captain. He had matured in one afternoon. Elizabeth and Peter and Helen were showier, but Charles became the steady one. They acknowledged him.

"Won't we wait for Mama?" Helen asked. "Did I only imagine that she would be with us when we left?"

"I think she will be with us, for a while," Charles said. "Phoebe Jane says for us to cast off at moonrise. I believe she knows of the other rising at about the same time, but she doesn't know the name of it. So we will go at moonrise, and Witchy will be with us at almost the same time."

They were all sure of that now. They knew many things by illumination.

They had a pretty good time of it that afternoon, celebrating all the accumulated deaths. They made happy Bagarthach verses with the very blood dripping out of them, and drank choc beer till they were all tipsy as a lilt of larks.

And in a peculiar rite they now shed their Earth names and assumed the Puca equivalents. This had to come of themselves. The group was now of an age to devise intuitively the names that were destined for them. Puca children are always given nicknames first, or in the case of the Puca of the *Eisimirce* (the Dispersal), native names of the place. They must, when the time comes, guess their real names, and they will do so if they are true Pucas. It is their Epiphany, their opening out.

Elizabeth realized herself as Coisreacan-Dia.

Charles assumed Laidir.

Peter was translated literally into Carraig.

Dorothy naturally was Feirin-De.

Helen was rekindled as Lochrann.

John was made manifest as Dia-Ta-Caomh.

And Bad John, of course, was to be called Ionuin.

They all realized Bad John's name now, but where was he himself?

"I think that Ionuin Bad John has gone too," Elizabeth said. "We haven't seen him for several hours."

"I believe he's gone for good," Carraig Peter said. So they made another bloody Bagarthach verse to celebrate the termination of Bad John as they had known him.

Just after dark, Phoebe Jane Lanyard came silently as a breeze and provisioned them.

"Leave at moonrise," she told them again. "I will have Witchy near, and she will join you as you move." Then Phoebe was gone.

"We should have a black sail," Lochrann Helen said. "Then we would be invisible at night."

Laidir Charles climbed the highest tree that overhung

the river and began his moon-vigil. The rest of them
waited below, and everything was shipshape.

When Charles saw the moon rising—no, actually when
he saw a faint body considerably to the south of it rise at
near the same time—he dived from the top of the tree and
cut the black water. He swam effortlessly to the *Ile* and
boarded it.

"Cast off!" he ordered. "Sound the ship's horn. Damn
the noise, this is symbolic."

They unlashed from the trees and poled themselves into
the stream, with the *Ile* in the lead and the *Sea Bear* in
tow. They headed perfectly and took the current. Then,
before they were out of the region of perpetual fog around
Misu Mound, and just where the current drags in very near
the left bank, Witchy was onto the craft as weightless as a
ghost.

"We are together now for a while," she said. "You
have a very long way to go, and I only a short one. I will
tell you a little if I can find the right words; but my head is
in the hockshop of this world, and I haven't the coin to
redeem it.

"There is on this world a most peculiar and remarkable
ethic. The people of this world fail it by not taking it
literally enough. Ourselves, if we try it, will fail it by
taking it too literally. A cousin of mine did this. He was
charmed by this ethic, and he resolved to follow it. He did
so for half a day.

"'If your right hand offend you, hack it off,' said the
ethic. It wasn't two minutes till his right hand offended,
and he hacked it off. 'If your eye offend, pluck it out.' I
tell you, his eye offended every time he blinked. It went
through the whole alphabet of his members and body. He
wasn't a bad fellow, for a Puca, but offensive he was in the
real sense. He offended from the crine of his head to the

metatarsus of his foot, and he hacked off every offending part. I will spare you the unglorious details. In two hours there was nothing left of him but the torso, and that was pretty well hacked up.

" 'If I'm going to Hell in a handbasket, it looks like I'm in a pretty good shape to start,' my cousin said. 'That's enough for one day. If I feel better I may try it again tomorrow.' I say it is a fine thing, but it was not given to us, and they to whom it was given have not taken it. I am not scoffing in this. We Pucas have so much going against us that we can never afford the bad manners of scoffing.

"Ourselves, we live by a more primitive ethic. We do not deny that it is primitive, but it is the only ethic that the Giver has given us yet. We will live that primitive ethic all the way. Be swift, and be sudden! That is our secret. You can chop down those wiser and more powerful than yourself while they are meting out their wisdom and power. They are the many fat rats. We are the few shrews. Well, let us be good at it since it's our role. I believe that the one who gives the Parting Admonition is also supposed to mention something about the responsibility attached to the thing, but my mind begins to wander."

"Mama," Lochrann Helen said, "Ionuin Bad John isn't with us. He isn't on either of the rafts. Is he gone?"

"Oh, he's gone with his father Frank. With us, small children are allowed to linger for a few years after they have died; but it isn't the custom on Earth. He was looking bad; I don't believe that the atmosphere here is very nourishing; now he'll be all right."

They were sliding down Green River in the slanting darkness, and they found it pleasant. Earth has a beauty even for the Pucas—at night, with the dog-elm and the crooked-neck cedar trees giving their smell to the setting and leaning out over the water, with the moon coming up over the shaggy little river, and the night cicadas talking—it is especially beautiful when seen through green eyes.

"Where will we go, Mama?" Lochrann Helen asked. (We will gradually grow accustomed to the new names; it takes a while.)

"Why, for a while you can go where the rivers go," Briochtog Witchy said. "The Green River flows into the Arkansas, and the Arkansas flows into the Mississippi, the biggest river in the world. All the other rivers run into it, the Red, the Missouri, the Nile."

"No, Mama not the Nile, that's in Egypt," Lochrann Helen said.

"Of course, dear. We lived up there one year. We used to call it Little Egypt. The Nile rolls into the Mississippi along about at Paducah, Kentucky. You'll find Cairo and Thebes and Shawneetown and a lot of other Egyptian places along there. I'm almost sure it's the Nile. If I'm wrong you have to make allowances for me; I've been officially classified as a filbert for a week now.

"You will have ten nights of moonlight to hatch your thoughts, and all the days will be sunny while you travel. Please understand that you can go anywhere you want to in this world. It all belongs to you now. I'd have loved such a trip myself."

"Won't you be with us?" Lochrann Helen asked.

"Oh no. The Earth Sickness has caught me," Briochtog Witchy said. "But it won't catch you. You were born on Earth and built up immunity early. Wasn't that clever of you? I will die tonight."

"That will be nice, Mama," Coisreacan-Dia Elizabeth said. "It's fun to bury people at early dawn on a river bank, and we'll have time to make up funny Bagarthach verses about it beforehand. I wish I had a red dress for the funeral. Mama, you look more and more like Aunt Veronica.''

"Old potato face and all," Witchy Briochtog laughed. "I know. This is how it should be. You know the banter line, 'Do you really look like that, or you just kidding?' Why, I've been kidding ever since I came to Earth. We all have been, to a degree. Let us all look like ourselves now and let the world be damned. Wouldn't it be funny if we became a fad and the World people tried to look like us?''

"Aunt Briochtog," Peter Carraig said (for Witchy had had her Puca name for longer than the children were old, and they were now permitted to call her by it), "I can see we're going to have quite a battle with it. Somebody better tell us when it's time to take the gloves off and handle this thing barehanded."

"It's time now, Carraig. For years we studied custom and tried to devise ways to live in accord with this World without changing it too much. We used up Gracious Understanding by the gallon and Patience by the long ton. But when you're sick and tired you run out of patience. This isn't just a personal thing; it is the condition that this World imposes on us seeders. I was already mad at this place when they killed my Henry. 'Forget it, forget it,' someone might say, but one element of the Earth Sickness is the inability to forget these trifles.

"There isn't any way to live in accord with this World as it is, children. You will have to chance it here and there, and sometimes you will have to excise elements that seem important to Earth people. It's a stubborn and worthless old animal the way it is. Break it.

"But your first idea of killing all the people, though it was perhaps in the right direction, was like something little children would think up. Now you will leave off being children, save for a while in appearance. Kill then when you feel the need of it, of course; but mostly you will control and alter till you see if something cannot be made of the place.''

"There isn't going to be any real gentle way to do it," Laidir Charles said. "I've got some pretty good ideas, though."

"Remember, you must be, in a real sense, the Salt of the Earth," Briochtog Witchy admonished them.

"Boy, I bet this was an insipid place before we came here," Lochrann Helen said. "If it weren't for us, I don't see how we could stand it at all."

"Let the World take its chances with you!" Briochtog Witchy cried. "We can protect it from you no longer. I break the egg! I turn you loose! Oh, my own Dragons' Seed!"

"I know that's an Earth phrase, mama," Lochrann Helen said, "but how did they know about us, that we would come?"

"I guess they just had a sneaky premonition of it," Witchy laughed. "And there's another phrase they have—'a plague of demons.' You aren't, but to them you will seem so. There's a tagline in an old joke, 'Pardon me, I gotta go die now.' Myself, I come to the joke literally.''

"It's all right, Mama, go ahead and do it. Don't give it another thought," Coisreacan-Dia Elizabeth said.

Six little pair of goblin eyes glowing green in the dark; and a seventh older pair nictitated by death slumber to a fainter green.

And opposed to them, only the defenseless World!

THE END

JOURNEY THROUGH MIND AND SPACE
WITH BERKLEY'S SF

TELEMPATH   (03548-4—$1.50)
  by Spider Robinson

THE CITY OUTSIDE   (03549-2—$1.50)
THE WORLD
  by Lin Carter

NIGHT OF LIGHT   (03366-X—$1.50)
  by Philip Jose Farmer

CHILDREN OF DUNE   (03310-4—$1.95)
  by Frank Herbert

THE 1978 DUNE CALENDAR   (03604-9—$4.95)
  by Frank Herbert & John Schoenherr

SURVIVAL RUN   (03123-3—$1.25)
  by Roger Zelazny

Send for a *free* list of all our books in print
_____

These books are available at your local bookstore, or send
price indicated plus 30¢ per copy to cover mailing costs to
Berkley Publishing Corporation
390 Murray Hill Parkway
East Rutherford, New Jersey 07073

THE CLASSIC SCIENCE FICTION
OF ROBERT HEINLEIN

FARNHAM'S FREEHOLD   (03568-9—$1.95)

GLORY ROAD   (03134-9—$1.75)

THE MOON IS A HARSH   (03436-4—$1.75)
MISTRESS

ORPHANS OF THE SKY   (03217-5—$1.25)

THE PAST THROUGH   (03178-0—$2.75)
TOMORROW

PODKAYNE OF MARS   (03434-8—$1.50)

STARSHIP TROOPERS   (03218-3—$1.50)

STRANGER IN A   (03067-9—$1.95)
STRANGE LAND

TIME ENOUGH FOR LOVE   (03471-2—$2.25)

TOMORROW THE STARS   (03432-1—$1.50)

THE UNPLEASANT PROFESSION (03052-0—$1.50)
OF JONATHAN HOAG

Send for a *free* list of all our books in print

These books are available at your local bookstore, or send
price indicated plus 30¢ per copy to cover mailing costs to
Berkley Publishing Corporation
390 Murray Hill Parkway
East Rutherford, New Jersey 07073

**POUL ANDERSON
IS PUBLISHED BY BERKLEY**

HOMEWARD AND BEYOND   (03162-4—$1.50)

SATAN'S WORLD   (03361-9—$1.50)

TAU ZERO   (03210-8—$1.50)

TRADER TO THE STARS   (03199-3—$1.25)

THE TROUBLE TWISTERS   (03245-0—$1.25)

Send for a *free* list of all our books in print

These books are available at your local bookstore, or send
price indicated plus 30¢ per copy to cover mailing costs to
Berkley Publishing Corporation
390 Murray Hill Parkway
East Rutherford, New Jersey 07073

ROBERT E. HOWARD'S
CLASSIC WORKS OF FANTASY

CONAN: THE HOUR OF THE DRAGON   (03608-1—$1.95)

CONAN: THE PEOPLE OF THE BLACK CIRCLE AND OTHERS   (03609-X—$1.95)

CONAN: RED NAILS AND OTHERS   (03610-3—$1.95)

Send for a *free* list of all our books in print

These books are available at your local bookstore, or send price indicated plus 30¢ per copy to cover mailing costs to
Berkley Publishing Corporation
390 Murray Hill Parkway
East Rutherford, New Jersey 07073